"The first and fundamental law of history is that it should neither dare to say anything that is false, nor fear to say anything that is true . . ." Cicero

INTO THE TWILIGHT

The True Origins of Abe Lincoln

An Historical Novel

Annis Ward Jackson

INTO THE TWILIGHT

The True Origins of Abe Lincoln

Copyright 2008 by Annis Ward Jackson

Cover art by Jim Finch

SunnyBrick Publishers

Author's Note

This book is not presented as a biography but as a work of fiction although many of the characters are real people. My goal was to extract a convincing sequence of events from the overwhelming body of traditional lore that exists on this subject. That lore owes its existence to many ordinary people who were close to the story, and to reputable nineteenth century judges, ministers, and attorneys and their followers who carried it into the twentieth and twenty-first centuries.

Acknowledgements:

I owe my gratitude to many people along the way, my mother who fostered my interest in words and reading, many excellent teachers, especially Dr. F. David Sanders who was director of the honors program and my adviser at East Carolina University.

I am especially grateful to my husband whose support has been essential and absolute in all my writing ventures.

Prologue

4 March 1861
Washington, D.C.

My Dear Mother,

*   I take pen in hand as though you were still alive
and   well at Pigeon Creek and waiting to hear from
me.   Would   that you could be here to share in my
victory at what I have for so long aspired to achieve.*

*   As I once said to my law partner, Herndon, I owe
everything I am to you, but since I was loath to
elaborate, I'm not sure he completely understood. It is
through your blood and the blood of my natural father
that I was granted the intellect, the wisdom, the
judgment, and all other attributes necessary to bring
me to where I am today. That knowledge sustains me
when despondency plunges me into a bottomless chasm
populated by all manner of ghosts and demons and
specters. Only to you can I speak of the cause of these
fits of melancholia.*

*   Dear Mother, only you and I know what cruelties
we suffered at the hands of Thomas Lincoln. If I must
admit to owing anything to him, it is my ability to
remain, even today, stoic and resolute in the face of
abuse of any kind.*

*   The necessity of continuing to allow the world to
believe that Thomas Lincoln, the lowest, crudest, and
basest of men, was my father galls my very soul, but
there it is. There is no cure. If I could see anything to
be gained, if it would benefit my country in any manner*

to know my true lineage, I would bespeak it tomorrow from the highest steps of the Capitol. Yet, to acknowledge it now would not only be political ruin for me but would be devastating to those who have supported me at great cost along the way, and indeed, destructive to our nation, especially at this time when such a great divisive storm has already begun to brew.

So, my Dear Mother, I must go on pretending about my ancestry, allowing others to believe what you and I, and the Enloes and Tanners know to be false. I gain some small comfort in the truth that dwells in my heart though I know it must always remain unspoken.

A knock interrupted the letter writer. The door opened and a young page entered.

"Mr. Lincoln? Mr. Lincoln, Sir. Justice Taney is waiting to administer the oath of office."

The page bowed slightly, backed away, and closed the door. The dark somber-faced man rose from the table, his head almost touching the exposed beams on the ceiling of the small anteroom. He moved over to the fireplace, laid the letter on the flames, and waited until it burned and fell into ashes. He bowed his head for a moment, then took his stovepipe hat from a peg on the wall and left the room.

Chapter One

<u>Abraham Enloe</u>

My family came to America in the mid-sixteen hundreds. They were proper Scots, Highlanders, not the Scotch-Irish rabble that followed a century later. I make this statement, not in a wholly disparaging manner, but to distinguish two sets of people who originated in the same country but who were foreign to each other in many ways, especially in their approaches to hard work. Yet, my ancestors were not really working men, at least not physical laborers.

They were well known and well respected schoolteachers. With the passage of several generations, the story of why two of the three Enloe brothers came to choose South Carolina instead of remaining in Maryland was lost. The great-grandson of one of these men, I passed my childhood in Charleston, South Carolina, but even then the city was no longer the tiny seaport it was when my ancestors arrived.

After several generations the Enloe appearance may have changed somewhat from marrying outside the family lines, but the importance of education never did. So, as a youngster, I studied like my father before me, and his before him. I was a good and attentive student, as I'm sure they had been, but in the same way my Scottish ancestors had heard stories of America and left their familiar surroundings to take up life in a new and exciting country, so did I hear talk of the wild and wonderful Appalachian mountains called so by Spanish explorer De Soto for the Applachee Indians he had encountered in the Florida Panhandle.

When my ancestors came to America, they sought a populated place where they could exercise their calling as educators. I had finished my education, at least the academic part of it, and could have taken up a vocation in many areas. Instead, I dreamed of the wild lands, the faraway places where no white man except maybe Daniel Boone had ever been.

By the time I was nineteen, I knew what course I wanted my life to take. Uncle Isaac, my father's eldest brother, owned land in western North Carolina on which he had paid quitrents for many years. Being of an already advanced age and not inclined to start life again in the wilderness, he sold me the land at a very reasonable price.

My family was loath to give me approval to make such a drastic move but when they realized that my mind was set, they quietly gave me their blessing along with a share of the family fortune to help smooth my way into the wilderness.

Yes, I answered my mother's query. I would miss Charleston in some ways. It was a familiar place filled with people from many cultures. It was called

Charles Town in the beginning for England's Charles the Second. Colonists directly from England and British colonists who had been several generations on the island of Barbados settled the area equally. The houses were mostly made of stone or brick, decreed so after the great fire of 1740, twenty years before I was born.

Many of the brick houses were influenced by the West Indies and covered with stucco, tinted soft hues of pink, blue, green, or yellow that created a fairyland appearance in the sunrise. Iron balconies and tiled roofs came with the French Huguenots who fled their homeland seeking religious tolerance.

Beautiful St. Michael's church was patterned after London's St. Martins-in-the-Field. A Library Society had been established in 1748 and two decades later, by the time I had need of its services, had accumulated a massive circulating collection.

But, really, what were these amenities to a young, healthy and energetic fellow whose sights were set on excitement and adventure in a wild and untamed land?

So, in the year of our Lord, 1779, I availed myself of all the accoutrements necessary, left Charleston with four loaded wagons, Moses and George, two slaves who would remain with me, and two of my father's bond servants who would return to Charleston with one of the wagons when I no longer required their services.

Rutherford County had an unlimited western boundary and only a short time before had been called Tryon. A new county named Lincoln had recently been created out of an eastern section of Tryon. The remainder had been renamed for a great Indian fighter, Griffith Rutherford, who would later become a member of the Provincial Congress and a Revolutionary War general.

William Tryon, for whom the area had originally been named, was a Tory. The North Carolina legislature had passed a Confiscation Act at the beginning of the year and vast sums of money drawn from sales of Tory property were already filling the state's coffers. I blessed my good fortune at having purchased mine from my uncle who was steadfastly and openly loyal to the cause of Independence from England.

Having been born in 1760, and the British having begun their oppressive taxation policies just three years later, I could not remember a time when our independence was not a topic of discussion. At least once a year, the British would apply some new form of taxation or repressive edict to the colonies and a rebellion of some sort would follow.

Our neighbors to the north reacted more strongly in the beginning, perhaps partly because they were closer to the center of activity than we further south, and partly because the Loyalist faction was much greater in our area. My mother, an educated and refined lady of Charleston society, was positively giddy when she received a missive from her cousin in Edenton, North Carolina in December of 1774 relating the story of fifty-one ladies who met and staged their own tea party, a mirror image of the one in Boston in December of the previous year. They vowed to purchase no more British tea and to wear no more British manufactured clothing.

According to Cousin Lizzie Nash, she accompanied the procession to the town square where the ladies solemnly laid their British tea "upon the inferno." Of course, we had heard of the dissension in Boston and it met with our resounding approval, but Cousin Lizzie's involvement gave added significance to the Edenton protest.

After the Revolution began in earnest, it proceeded at what seemed to a young man a lumbering pace. Then, in December of 1778, Tory troops moved south, captured Savannah, Georgia, and restored Royal rule. With much conversation about the possibilities, we waited their arrival in Charleston. It was not to happen until after I had left for Rutherford in late October of 1779.

Our small train left Charleston and traveled northwest to Columbia where we entered an ancient Indian trading trail called the Occaneechi Path that was already being referred to as the Georgia Road. We entered North Carolina and passed through Charlottesburgh and remained on the same trail until we reached Bryant's Settlement in the South Yadkin.

We drove our wagons into a fenced area in the Settlement belonging to a Mr. Bryan with whom I had previously corresponded on the subject of leasing the space for the winter. I would board in a private home and compensate yet another farmer to accommodate my two slaves and two bondsmen for the winter.

It was at the dinner table of my hosts, the Carters, that I heard the news that Daniel Boone and his party of settlers had left the Yadkin for Kentucky just a little more than a month before. What a disappointment, and yet, what a thrill to be in essence following the great man's example by going into my own wilderness.

I passed the winter, the coldest the Yadkin settlers had ever experienced, reading during the coldest days and riding and walking for exercise on the warmer, the latter activity amusing my hosts exceedingly. Leaving the Yadkin in early March of 1780, we took Sherrill's Path and then Island Ford Road southwest and arrived three weeks later in Rutherford.

I was there for nearly three months before hearing that Cornwallis had captured my birth city a month earlier in May. I was distracted by the possibilities of the hardships my family might be enduring but not so much that I ignored my dedication to my new life in the wilderness.

The land I acquired from my uncle lay in the Eastern part of Rutherford County about ten miles southwest of a tiny settlement called Puzzle Creek which had grown up at the head of Puzzle Creek, a small but rushing waterway. Puzzle Creek, named so for quicksand that caused the earliest settlers to wonder if they could cross it, ran southwest into a river called the Second Broad, the First Broad lying a few miles east near the Lincoln County line.

The few settlers around Puzzle Creek owned very small tracts of land, many less than fifty acres. Few, if any, entertained the idea of moving further west to obtain more acreage, although there was still much available. Fresh in their memories were the Cherokee attacks instigated by the British just three years before, which left a trail of dead and wounded and entire settlements burned to the ground.

A treaty with the Cherokee had been signed a year after Captain Thomas Howard led a force of colonial militia and several hundred Catawba Indians, who were longtime foes of the Cherokees, across the area. They not only pushed them back but also destroyed everything in their path until the Cherokees surrendered.

I had no experience with the natives but I had heard enough over the years from the fur trappers who brought their wares to Charleston to understand the settler's lack of enthusiasm for moving further west.

My holding of five hundred acres was massive compared to theirs and I soon found myself in the position of major landowner and promptly stirred the ire of some of the less fortunate residents who seemed to resent my ability to pay craftsmen to build my home.

However, I had always liked and been tolerant of my fellow man until I had true reason not to, so I bore them no ill will and went about my business of finding enough hearty young men who, along with those I brought with me, would begin building a cabin on my property as soon as I had duly explored it and chosen the best site.

I selected an area about ten miles from Puzzle Creek. An old trail, likely made by Indians and animals, which began at the edge of my property, led nearly to the site. There were long stretches where very little work was necessary for a wagon to pass. It took three days to clear the other places and then, there we were, ready to go to work.

The cabin would be built in a sort of level spot at the base of a hollow where two mountainsides would partially block the cold winter winds. The front would face the morning sun. Water ran down from a generous spring and there was plenty of wood on the surrounding slopes that could be easily dragged down for fuel.

The young laborers in my employ were openly astonished at the size of the foundation I laid out, declaring that no one in the settlement had built a cabin of anywhere near that size. They were rendered speechless when I later informed them that the structure would also have an upper floor of equal footage. Moses and George knew me well enough to simply nod and smile.

Good poplars, limbless, and therefore knotless, grew near the site and yielded easily to the excellent tools I had brought from Charleston. Before long, word of my house had reached the ears of the settlers and every few days a small group, mostly men, would show up to stand and stare in awe.

Upon arrival, I had constructed for myself a camp or shelter, called a half-face, the kind I had heard described by fur traders from Cherokee country who had gathered at a warehouse belonging to my father. They told grand tales of heroic ventures and Indian wives but there was practical knowledge there for anyone who would listen. And I had listened.

I searched and found a large rock cliff that jutted outward at just such an angle that I could stand long sapling birch poles on the ground and then lean them against the rock face. Alternating the large and small ends closed up the cracks quite nicely. About fifty of these poles made a substantial wall and resulted in a room of about eight by eight feet.

Then I cut piles and piles of white pine limbs heavy with needles. Laying them in rows and securing them with leather strips, starting at the foot of the poles and working up in thatched roof fashion, I soon had a relatively dry shelter. I could fit my entire six-foot four-inch frame on the ground and sleep comfortably on my straw pallet.

The shelter was useless, of course, against assault from wild beasts such as mountain lions, black bears, or wolves all of which were common in the area, but my loaded musket and pistol and a well-honed poll axe were always near at hand.

Moses and George and the two bondservants slept in the wagons that had held mostly tools, cooking utensils and other items that were needed for building. The men from Puzzle Creek slept beside the fire, rolled in blankets.

My hired helpers knew more about appropriate wood than I, so when we needed a stone boat, or sled, to transport stones, I left them to it. They built it large and sturdy with runners made of ash, which they said would wear better than any other wood while being dragged over the rocky ground.

For six days, one of the bondservants who had experience as a mason carefully chose stone after stone, fitting them together, chinking them tightly with a mixture of clay and straw until suddenly there was a spacious fireplace and a tall chimney that extended several feet beyond the rafters above the second story. He built a matching one at the opposite end.

My young crew again expressed their wonder as I set two of them to using a whipsaw to rive thick boards for the floors. A whipsaw is a long two-man saw positioned vertically in a heavy woodrack built over a pit in the ground.

One man worked above, the other below as the sharp teeth cut through the logs and eventually transformed them into a stack of thick floorboards. Because the boards were not of an exact thickness, appropriate grooves were chopped out with an adze where they crossed the floor joists to create a reasonably level surface.

We used chestnut shakes on the roof because the tree was plentiful, and easily felled, cut and split. The sharp crack of an almost perfect slab of chestnut separating from a massive block was a satisfying sound. Laid on in overlapping rows starting from the east, we covered the roof ridge with wider shingles for more protection against the winter winds.

At times I felt as if we had been working for months instead of weeks, but we forged ahead and suddenly one day the house was finished. The sheer size was impressive to my hired helpers but in addition, glass paned windows carefully packed and brought by wagon from Charleston adorned the front, evenly balanced with two on each side of the door and two on each side of the upper story.

The window openings at each end and in the back of the house were equipped with simple wooden shutters that could be opened to the inside and secured for daytime, then closed at night. The great stone chimneys at each end stood like sentinels watching over all they surveyed. It was not a Charleston house but it was one of which my workmen and I could be proud.

There was much congratulating and back patting among my workmen. They would have stories to tell their families and friends on their return to Puzzle Creek. I also was ready for a change of pace. Late summer was upon us and there was still time to raise the outbuildings I would need: springhouse, privy, a small barn for storing tools and providing shelter for my two best riding horses and a cabin for Moses and George.

According to my foreman, an energetic and trustworthy fellow named Jacob Harman whom I intended to take on permanently if he was willing, informed me that several of the settlers in Puzzle Creek planned a festivity of sorts to welcome any newcomers to the area. I had been in Rutherford since late March, and although I thrived on the hard physical work and the clean open air, I was ready for the society of more than my hired hands.

I found appropriate clothing packed away in a trunk that remained on one of the wagons. They were very plain garments by Charleston standards but I had no doubt they would suffice here with more simple folk.

The Edgertons owned the largest house in Puzzle Creek and the people gathered there were of such a number that I thought they must have come from surrounding settlements. Then I realized that I had been counting houses and not people. Children ranged from five to twelve per family. The Edgertons alone had ten, the eldest but one a delightful young lady who caught my attention immediately.

Her name was Sarah and while her hairstyle and manner of dress was far from what I was accustomed to seeing in Charleston, I could not help but think that with very little change she could hold her own beside any South Carolina belle. I determined that I would do well to know her better and asked to be presented.

She wore a russet linsey-woolsey gown with a white lace collar, delicately tatted even though it had been made with coarse cotton thread. She was taller than the average woman but she held her shoulders straight and moved with self-confidence unusual in someone her age.

When my name was given, she tossed her head slightly, just enough to rustle a wondrous generosity of auburn curls. Her clear green eyes struck me speechless with their unflinching gaze. After what seemed a very long silence, while in truth it was but a few moments, I spoke.

"Miss Edgerton? Your servant, Ma-am."

She gave me her hand and I felt a strength that I had never known in a woman's hand before. She spoke and her voice was a bit throaty, not hoarse, but with a quality that says the speaker is slightly amused.

"Mr. Enloe…welcome to our home."

From that moment I felt as if we were the only two people in the room. There were many more who sought to make my acquaintance but as the evening progressed, I hardly remembered my words to any of them.

Every moment my eyes sought her in the crowd and I made every move in her direction so that I could speak with her at any opportunity, however brief.

"Your cabin, Mr. Enloe, rather, your house…how will you furnish it?"

Before I could answer sensibly, someone dragged me away to meet the circuit magistrate who was in the area briefly, Puzzle Creek being a part of his territory. The remainder of the evening, when Sarah Edgerton and I met, our conversations began where we had left them, as if we had never been separated.

By the end of the evening, I was desperately in love with this green-eyed auburn-haired vision who seemed equally adept at conversation, serving food and drink to her father's guests, or settling a quarrel between two of her younger siblings.

By pure blind habit I mounted my horse later that evening and was miles down the trail when I realized that I had little memory of the other people I had met. Conversations with anyone except Sarah Edgerton were but vague and insignificant recollections while each word she had spoken remained sharp and clear in my head.

Back in my shelter I lay with hands behind my head far into the night, remembering her green eyes, the way she moved through the crowd smoothly and assuredly, and how her voice had thrilled me like no other girl I had ever met. Before I finally slept, I determined to further our acquaintance at the first opportunity. Little did I know what adventure awaited me before seeing her again.

The sky was still dark the next morning when hoof beats awakened me. I crawled from my shelter in time to see one of the Puzzle Creek fellows who had worked for me entering the yard at a full gallop. While his horse watered at the trough, he explained his presence.

Some weeks before, Colonel Ferguson of the British army had sent aides to many mountain settlements, including Gilbert Town in Rutherford County, announcing imperiously that if the mountain patriots did not lay down their arms, *"he would march his forces over the mountains, hang their leaders, and lay waste to their country with fire and sword."*

Word had spread like wildfire. Arthur Sevier and Isaac Shelby had left Sycamore Shoals in Tennessee and come through Roan Mountain and Gillespie Gap with three hundred men. Their force had swollen to seven hundred and fifty when Joseph and Charles McDowell joined them at Quaker Meadows near Morganton.

They had picked up more on their way south and were now encamped in Lincoln County, just across the line from Rutherford. Sevier had sent runners to nearby settlements in order to increase his ranks before pursuing Ferguson.

After giving Moses and George and the two bond servants instructions about what should be done in my absence, I hastily packed saddle bags with food and ammunition, mounted my horse, a pistol in my belt and a musket in hand, and accompanied the runner back to Puzzle Creek.

The settlement was all-astir and the rising sun glinted off the barrels of a variety of firearms as a throng of men, young and old, readied themselves to answer Sevier and Shelby's call to arms. My heart raced with anticipation at what lay ahead.

I was no soldier but this was an opportunity for me to serve our new government and to seek vengeance for the damage my parents had sustained at the hands of Cornwallis in Charleston.

Some of the Puzzle Creek women were going from father to son saying goodbye and stuffing small parcels of food in their saddlebags or knapsacks. I did not see Sarah Edgerton but as we made the last turn out of the settlement I looked back and thought I caught a glimpse of auburn curls in the morning sun.

Finally, in a reasonably orderly fashion, we followed the small recruitment party away from Puzzle Creek, arrived at the camp in early afternoon and were greatly surprised at the size of the force. Nearly nine hundred men comprised our army, most like me with no military training but patriots who did not intend to bow before Ferguson or his king.

Scouts informed us late in the evening on October sixth, that Colonel Ferguson and his eleven hundred British soldiers were encamped on a bald mountain that lay almost on the North and South Carolina line. We approached the mountain the next morning and Shelby and Sevier divided us into four groups and gave us our orders. I don't remember seeing a single man with a distracted or frightened look on his face.

We fought Indian fashion from ambuscade barely allowing ourselves to be visible to the British. They fought entirely in the open in straight lines, and as the front line fell, another rose to take its place.

Repeated cries from my fellow fighters of "Tarleton's quarters! Tarleton's quarters!" was later explained to me. Lt. Col. Banastre "Bloody" Tarleton, a Tory cavalry commander, had sealed his reputation in the past few years in North Carolina where he made it a point to never take prisoners but to lay waste the land and the population, including women and children.

Incredibly, what we had thought might be a battle for many days turned out to be a short-lived skirmish that was over in an astonishing ninety minutes. After the guns fell silent and the smoke faded, one hundred and fifty British soldiers, including Colonel Ferguson, lay dead.

When their leader fell, the British force became a shambles. Unlike "Bloody Tarleton" we did take prisoners. Our army of mostly untrained militia captured one thousand British soldiers; our losses numbered only twenty-eight.

Sevier and Shelby's men took charge of the prisoners and the rest of us were free to go after the officers graciously expressed their gratitude and delight at what had been accomplished that day by men who had never trained as soldiers for a single day in their lives.

Those of us from Rutherford left our fellow fighters in Lincoln County and headed west for Puzzle

Creek. Our group had suffered no casualties but even so there was not a lot of merriment among us.

Weary, dirty, and longing for hot food and a comfortable bed, I did not tarry in Puzzle Creek but kept riding until I reached my property. Moses had moved my straw pallet into the house and a pot of hot venison stew awaited me on the hearth. That night I slept more soundly without the possibility of sharing my bed with some wild creature.

When I awoke the next morning, the entire episode seemed unreal somehow, as if I had only dreamed it. Then I arose and felt the stiffness in my body from days of riding and nights of sleeping on the ground.

Still, I felt at loose ends and assuming that my Puzzle Creek helpers likely felt the same, I decided to scout the areas of my property that I had not yet seen instead of returning immediately to building.

For most of three days I explored. I found valuable stands of hardwoods and almost every hollow was the outlet for a rushing stream. The larger creeks were full of trout.

Here and there through the forest were meadows of sometimes twenty or more acres, thick with a tender grass that my horse found very palatable. I surmised by the remains of charred stumps that the land had some years before been burnt over.

One of the Puzzle Creek fellows had told me how the Cherokees set fire to huge areas to let in more sun and encourage low plant growth that in turn would attract wild game. Large, healthy white tail deer roamed in herds and numerous flocks of turkeys gathered under the oaks to scoop up a new crop of acorns.

Wallows so large they must have been created by buffalo lay here and there in the meadows although I saw none of the creatures. Small game was plentiful and red squirrels that my laborers called Boomers chattered as they jumped from tree to tree.

Beautiful mushrooms grew on fallen logs and stumps, and up the bumpy trunks of ancient oaks. The French Huguenots in Charleston went on long forays to the surroundings woodlands to find and pick these fungi. I would not disturb them for I had been told that some were deadly and only an expert could distinguish the edible from the poisonous.

The northwestern corner of my property I found to be mountainous but not ruggedly so. Wide valleys with ample streams lay between the peaks. I would not have difficulty in finding areas to grow corn and tobacco to sell, and other vegetables for my family's subsistence and still leave undisturbed several hundred acres for wild game.

The thought of family brought sweet Sarah Edgerton to mind. She was a rare girl with none of the pretenses that was so prevalent in the girls I had known in Charleston. She would be an equal partner, not an adornment to wear on one's arm. I was sure I had the means to make her happy.

The money given me by my family on my departure would allow me to construct the necessary outbuildings, purchase breeding stock, horses, cows, swine and fowl, and still furnish our home in a comfortable manner. I would hire some of the furniture built locally but would order some from Charleston.

Considerable time would be required for the journey but having some of the niceties such as a linen press, wardrobes and chests for extra bed covers, and an armoire for our clothing would be worth waiting for.

"Good Lord!"

I spoke aloud and startled my horse that had almost fallen asleep while I daydreamed. Here I was having us already living in the house and I had not asked her father, and more importantly, her, to marry me.

The next day found me back home and of a mind to start work again. The following morning my Puzzle Creek helpers showed up and within a few hours we had laid the foundation for a springhouse. We framed it with locust and sided it with sturdy linden tree poles.

This was a species of tree that I had not known in Charleston and the men explained to me that it was not only good for building but that many people cut down the trees in surrounding forests because they sprouted many new tender branches that free-range cattle and hogs could forage upon.

We roofed the springhouse with chestnut boards and one of the men, who had done this kind of building before, hollowed out a half of a large poplar log as though he were making a canoe. This we settled on a bed of stones inside the building.

Then we rived some long boards, pegged them together to make a conduit that would channel the water from a small pond below the spring through an opening in the wall and into the log basin. After a few days the boards would swell and become watertight.

As the log filled up the water overflowed at the low end, dribbled down to a flat stone, on to the outside and back to its stream. Our milk and butter would stay cool and fresh here in the summer and in the winter a table would hold salted and dried meat.

A barn was next, which, like the springhouse we constructed by laying large trimmed and notched logs for the foundation, framing it with locust and siding it with linden tree poles, every other one reversed to fill the space evenly. We gave a generous pitch to the roof to make space for a hayloft.

We divided the ground space into stalls for my two best riding horses and a feed and tool room. I remembered well some words from the uncle from whom I had purchased my property.

"Remember, boy. All that separates us from the animals is our ability to create and use tools. Take care of your tools and they'll take care of you."

The other members of my strictly Scots-Presbyterian family would have cringed to hear Uncle Isaac's comparison of humans to animals but I took his words to heart and covered the tool room walls with wooden pegs and wide shelves to hold everything from horse harness to hammers and saws.

We built a two-room cabin with a fireplace for Moses and George, a much larger accommodation than they had in Charleston. Moses, whom I had known all my life, was delighted to have his own spacious garden where he could grow "tu-nips an' greens."

The privy was next. We built it a little distance away and slightly below the house in a grove of young locusts. My workmen had a good cackle at my expense when I called it by a proper Charleston name, *"House of Office."*

Two days later I was back in Puzzle Creek and speaking to Mr. Edgerton about wedding his daughter. He seemed favorably impressed by what he had heard of my means and my industrious nature. He readily gave his consent and then, all at once, all that was left was to speak to Sarah whom I found in the garden harvesting the last of the Rhubarb.

I could not find my voice. Thankfully, I did not actually stutter but the noise coming from my mouth did not sound much like words.

"Sarah, Sarah, will you…I would like…will you marry me?"

"Of course," she said, that enigmatic amusement barely visible on her face. "Of course I will. I thought you'd never get around to asking."

We were married in April, the next spring. By that time, everything was in place on the farm. Sarah brought her dowry chest filled with hand woven linens and quilts, a small wooden box of garden and flower seeds, and a cherry mantle clock made for her by a friend of her family after our banns were read in the settlement church.

Sarah took to life on the farm as if she had been schooled for it. The house, garden, and springhouse were her realm; mine was all the rest. She ruled with a firm hand all who dwelt there but was always just.

Our first child was born twenty-three months later, a daughter we named Nancy for my mother.

The following years brought many changes for us. Our farm prospered through hard work, persistence, faith in God, and of course, I was always aware that, unlike most of the settlers, I had started with good resources.

I did not consider myself a planter but yet did not fit the description of a simple farmer. We learned early that it was best all around to sell livestock on the hoof. Sometimes on the way to markets in the Yadkin or even Augusta, cattle would actually gain weight from grazing in lush grassy areas and hogs would eat their weight in acorns and chestnuts that tended to sweeten and tenderize their flesh.

The scarcity of salt during the war made preserving meat difficult and so added to the numbers of people who drove their cattle and hogs directly to markets. We had much fewer losses than many of our neighbors who continued to slaughter their livestock. Even well salted beef and pork could quickly become rancid on a market trip in unusually warm weather.

We raised most of our own food but we also profited from our excess, and made a tidy sum each year from the sale of corn and other produce that we could market locally or trade in the settlements.

We came to own the only forge and gristmill in the area and so kept in constant touch with the growing settlement. I was appointed a civil magistrate for our area.

A large group of settlers had come down from eastern Virginia in eighty-seven, many of them to own their own land for the first time. They settled in various places in Rutherford and became a part of our world on the edge of a wilderness.

Another addition was made to our family in seventeen ninety-three, a young servant girl so quiet in nature that sometimes it was easy to forget she was there.

Her mother was a weaver who roamed from farm to farm, weaving flax and wool into a cloth called linsey-woolsey, a tough fabric that stood up well to rough wear. The mother's name was Lucy Hanks and although her business on the farm was Sarah's realm, she approached me on her arrival one autumn day.

With her was a child, a girl, whom she held tightly by the shoulder as if she feared it would escape. The child was ten years old, the same age as our Nancy, although much slighter in size.

The long and short of it was that Lucy Hanks had never been married, thus putting her daughter in an irregular position. She sought to place her in our home as a servant. I, seeing no benefit to be had from such a slight creature, turned the matter over to Sarah.

To my surprise, she agreed to take the child on, saying that not only could she be a great help in easing some of the domestic concerns, she could share the burden with our Nancy of looking after the five younger children, the smallest of whom was not yet walking.

For my part, I insisted on making the agreement legal for I could anticipate the problems encountered if in a year or two her mother showed up and summarily removed her from our presence.

Whereas a child named Nancy, father unknown, born of Lucy Hanks, unmarried, be bound to Abraham and Sarah Enloe until she arrive at the age of 21 years, she being now about 10 years old. Abram Enloe agrees to provide said Nancy Hanks sufficient diet, clothing, and lodging, and shall teach or cause her to be taught to read and write a legible hand, and further to cause her to be taught the arts of housekeeping. Upon release from her bond, said Nancy Hanks will be provided suitable clothing and coin to maintain herself until able to become established in another position or situation. Signed: Abraham Enloe   Signed: Lucy Hanks

Sarah's only stipulation was that Lucy Hanks not be hired to weave on our farm again as it might be a distraction for the child to see her mother each year and face her leaving. I agreed and charged my foreman to be on the alert for a new weaver for the next season.

The girl's name being Nancy, we decided that to distinguish between them, our daughter would continue to be called simply Nancy, and the other by her first and last names, Nancy Hanks. And so she was.

The two Nancys took to each other right away and no caution from Sarah could discourage our daughter from treating the girl as if she were her own sister. They remained best of friends and Nancy Hanks became a part of the family, taking her schooling along with our brood and learning to dance and tat and cook and chatter with our Nancy and her sisters. She was bright and learned both her lessons and her manners almost as if she came by them naturally.

I could not help but speculate that her father must have been of some quality for I saw little of Lucy Hanks about her. Still, she earned her keep, never being far away when her mistress needed assistance.

More than once I remembered my grounds for the Bond agreement and was certain I had made a good judgment. After only a few months our Nancy would have been devastated by Nancy Hank's removal from our household, and Sarah would certainly have missed her competent assistance.

In 1791, our Rutherford County had been divided and along with a part of Burke County, made into a new county called Buncombe. Our lives were changed but little by the new borders but it was a sign that our wilderness world was becoming smaller, and therefore more crowded.

In 1799, we were inundated by many hundreds of fortune seekers when gold was discovered in the area. Our wilderness was disappearing into the fog of civilization and we were helpless to slow it down.

Then, one day in 1803 we looked up and realized that another great change had occurred. Our Nancy was nineteen and greatly infatuated with a young man from Kentucky by way of the Yadkin Settlements, a Moravian who had left his faith and went out on his own.

Arthur Thompson was handsome and smiling and without any means whatever, except for friends and a few thousand acres that awaited him in Kentucky, or as frontiersman Boone had first called it,

'Kan-tuk.' Thompson had stopped in Puzzle Creek to visit relatives and decided to tarry a while, as we learned later from Nancy Hanks, because he had met our Nancy.

We had naught against the young man personally, as he was of an amiable nature and appeared to be honest, industrious, and somewhat a gentleman. We simply thought our Nancy not mature enough to embark on marriage and a life of hardship in the wilderness.

Apparently, Nancy disagreed. In July, two months after her nineteenth birthday, she eloped with him, stopping at Duncan's Creek long enough for the Baptist minister, Reverend Swabel, to perform the marriage ceremony.

Her confederate, Nancy Hanks, accompanied her that far and then returned to a household in an uproar. Her quiet explanation was that she knew our Nancy was intent upon eloping with Mr. Thompson and she traveled with them far enough to make sure they were properly married.

We were greatly distressed for a while, I more than Sarah, but as the days wore on, we consoled ourselves with the fact that our Nancy was, indeed, properly married and to a good-seeming sort of man about whom we had yet to hear a negative word.

Sarah Edgerton

I knew from the first moment I saw Abraham Enloe across the room in my father's house that I would marry him someday. All that was left was, how? I remember thinking, 'What if he doesn't notice me?' But he did, and I felt his eyes on me the rest of the evening, even when my back was turned.

Abram, as he would later ask me to call him, stood nearly a head above any other man in the room. His body was muscular but his shoulders were those of a gentleman, not exactly narrow but yet not broad and bulging like the common laborers in our settlement. He carried himself well and did not stoop like many taller men are wont to do. His hair was black as a raven's wing, not curly but with a decided wave that gave it a pleasing texture.

The summer out of doors had lightly tanned his long serious face and a spot of color had settled on each high cheekbone. But, his deep-set eyes were what held my attention. They were not too large for his face but the dark gray pupils seemed to be larger than normal and there was a sparkle in them that never dimmed whether he was looking at me or speaking with my father or brothers.

I must admit I felt a twinge of resentment when I saw that same sparkle as he was introduced to Esther Battle, one of my friends. But I scolded myself and resolved that the light in his eyes was what first drew me to him and without its presence he would not be the same.

A few days later, Abram went back to his holdings to continue his building. I caught only a glimpse of him when he came to Puzzle Creek and joined the militia to help defeat Colonel Ferguson at King's Mountain. But, his place was not so very far away and there were fragments of news from time to time when one or another of his helpers came to the settlement for supplies.

The hardwoods had turned to red and rust and gold, the oaks had begun to drop their acorns, and chestnuts lay thickly on the ground when Abram returned to the settlement. Before noon of the second day, I looked out to see him tying his horse to our gatepost.

My cheeks were warm with anticipation as I fled to the back of the house. His and my father's voices intermingled but I could not make out a word they were saying although there was comfort in the fact that they were not loud.

I was in the garden pulling the last of the season's Rhubarb when he approached. I could hardly wait to hear what he was trying to say and I said yes before he had finished asking.

My father's condition on giving us his consent to marry was that we wait until spring so my first months of married life would not be spent many miles from home in what might be a harsh winter. I have always suspected that his intention was that we become better acquainted and know by spring whether our feelings were still the same.

Abram rode his horse in to the settlement several times that winter and took his meals with us. Just before Christmas, he arrived with a stone boat full of red-berried holly that we used to decorate our house.

Father remembered Old Christmas in England from where he came as a young boy. He had told us of the mummers and carolers and the roasted boar's heads and large bowls of spiced ale and wine. But we celebrated in a more simple fashion with venison and roast wild turkey, vegetables from our kitchen garden and fresh baked potato bread and puddings.

Our mother retained an ancient family receipt for a dark cake, heavy with dried apples and cherries, hickory nuts and walnuts, and flavored with rum. After our meal, we all went outdoors where Father, my brothers and many other young men fired their guns into the air in way of celebration. I enjoyed our festivities but I was anxious for spring.

After what seemed like an exceedingly long winter, although my father assured me repeatedly that it was the same length as the last one, April arrived, our banns were published and we were married at the small log church in Puzzle Creek.

I arrived at the farm with my dower chest and clothes, a box of vegetable and herb seeds, a small crate of rhubarb and asparagus roots, a bag of seed potatoes, a set of butter molds that had belonged to my maternal grandmother, and a cherry wood mantel clock made for us by my father's old friend, Josiah Duncan, the settlement's only skilled furniture builder.

Although I had heard much talk of the farm from Abram and others who had worked for him, I was unprepared for what lay before me when our wagon rounded the last bend.

The house was even larger than I had been told, indeed, considerably more spacious than the one I had just left. Abram helped me down and called for Moses to take care of the team, while he unloaded my belongings.

The interior of the house was a wondrous affair. Besides the spaciousness, every room had the necessary furniture, some of which I recognized as being from Josiah Duncan's hand, the rest of such a quality it had obviously come from Charleston.

The kitchen was also large. A` deep, wide fireplace with an elevated hearth almost covered one wall and was already hung with kettles and pots and skillets of varying sizes and all manner of meat forks, ladles, colanders and tongs. A Welsh cupboard filled most of the opposite wall and held a set of dishes with a blue pattern laid on, that I could see were unequaled by any others in Puzzle Creek.

Four bedrooms were unheard of, but there they were. Each bed was dressed with two feather mattresses, one for under, one for over, plus plump feather pillows. On the end of the house opposite the kitchen was a parlor with the same large fireplace, capable, I was to learn, of accepting a log of nearly five feet.

That Abram had chosen wisely in the location of the house was obvious. A less conscientious man might have made his choice based on where the house could have been easiest built.

The springhouse was not far from the kitchen, just past a large square that Abram had spaded up and fenced with pole pickets for a vegetable and herb garden. There I planted the rhubarb and asparagus roots in deep hills. I cut the seed potatoes into pieces with at least two eyes.

Our climate was too cool and our growing seasons too short here in Rutherford for the sweet potatoes that Abram had been accustomed to in Charleston. I raked and laid out rows for the vegetable seeds I had brought with me and marked them with sticks. I would plant them as soon as the threat of frost had passed.

Abram had brought back breeding stock, horses, cows, and hogs, on his trips to the Yadkin. Among them was a cow that Moses milked each morning and evening.

It was with great satisfaction that I churned, salted and pressed the butter into my grandmother's molds, then turned out the rounds to reveal the perfect imprint of a tulip on each one. The water in the springhouse kept the butter, buttermilk, and sweet milk fresh and cold.

Father and Mother visited in July and we spoke at length of the war and speculated on how much longer it might last. We raised a beaker of cider in salute to our country's independence.

Our first summer was like a whirlwind, here, and then suddenly gone. Fall was just as challenging. Not only did food have to be preserved for the human inhabitants of our farm, but for the animals as well.

Abram knew that many farmers simply turned out their stock for the winter, hoping they could forage enough to maintain them until spring. But that was neither his way nor his nature. Indeed, the practice offended him greatly.

The bondservants had mowed and hauled in grass from the outlying areas since mid-summer, knowing that they were due to leave for Charleston in September. Abram had planted a large, very successful corn crop. After the ears were gathered and stored in a crib, he cut the cornstalks and stood them in shocks to use as fodder for the cattle.

With each hill of corn had gone two beans and in every tenth hill a pumpkin seed. Earlier in the summer I had strung and dried any beans we could not eat fresh. I did the same with the pumpkins, cutting them into cubes that I strung up and hung near the kitchen fireplace to dry.

George tended several hives of bees that he kept near his cabin for protection, for bears would rip them to shreds in search of even a taste of honey. When sourwoods bloomed there was a constant hum of bees flying out rapidly and then returning slowly, their bodies almost weighted down by the golden pollen that would be turned into honey.

George built birch wood boxes and sealed them with beeswax. In these we stored our only source of sweetener. I loved the golden syrup so much that, like a child, I could not resist dipping my finger into the flowery nectar and allowing the sweetness to spread over my tongue. George taught me to mix honey, whiskey and thyme to make a soothing sore throat medicine that was to come in handy many times over the years.

Abram decided that we must have a root cellar so his men dug a long rectangle back into a steep bank, lined the three walls with poles and covered the top with split logs. Thick sods placed close together on the roof and a thick door on the front kept our potatoes, cabbage, turnips, carrots, and several bushels of apples Abram bought in Puzzle Creek, from freezing. I dried a wealth of herbs and stored them in a series of small wooden boxes that had once held pipe tobacco.

I went back to Puzzle Creek only once that first year. The circuit minister was to preach at the log church where Abram and I were married. We attended church and then went to my father's house for dinner.

Afterward, my sister and I walked about the settlement and visited many of my childhood friends. The visit was pleasant but I was pleased when we arrived home the next day. Somehow I had come to think of our farm as a kind of Eden, a blasphemous thought, I suppose, but one that gave me great pleasure.

Abram had scarcely gotten the last load of corn in his crib when winter was upon us. The first snow stayed on the ground for nearly six weeks. The water running into the springhouse froze solid but the spring continued to flow and the ponds in the creek remained open for the livestock. Our root cellar did its job and neither we nor Moses and George wanted for ample food.

The winter had its chilling moments, though. Late one night, Abram's dog, a large hound he had bought from a Mr. Plott, began to bark and growl. Abram ran from the house with a pitch light and his gun.

A large black bear was trying to rip his way into the springhouse where our winter's supply of meat was stored. The barking dog and two shots from Abram's gun were sufficient to chase the beast away.

Then, there were the nights that we could hear panthers on the ridges above us. Their screams faded in and out as they move from place to place. Now and then we would hear wolves howling but they never came near the house.

I thought of Moses and George and wondered if they felt the same as I about the almost human screams and howls. Sometimes when Abram sat up by the fireside to read from one of the many books he had brought from Charleston, I would try to imagine that I was alone. I could not, for already he was as much a part of me as my heart or my soul and I could not imagine life without him.

Suddenly spring was upon us. We had survived, well fed and none the worse for our three months of near hibernation. The trees began to bud, grass began to green, and willows along the creek banks started to display their silvery catkins. Intricately folded rhubarb leaves began to unfurl and one day I went out to find crispy green spears of asparagus covering the mounded row where I had planted the roots the previous spring.

Abram's stock was in reasonably good shape. Two of his seven hogs were missing, likely taken by panthers or bears, but the cows and horses had fared well with regular feedings of fodder, hay and corn.

Through letters from Abram's family we learned that our new government and Britain had signed a preliminary peace agreement in November, but it was a nervous peace and some fighting continued in remote areas of the country where the news did not reach.

To make the year of seventeen eighty-three a memorable one, a final treaty was signed with the British in September making us a truly independent nation. Abram talked at length about the wrinkles a new country would need to iron out.

His education and never-ending need to be informed sometimes made me feel a bit inferior but that feeling quickly passed when I reminded myself of his good and generous nature. Abram was ever concerned with my health and insisted that I worked too hard.

As a result, he was always creating something that would make my work easier or more convenient. In Puzzle Creek, at my father's home, were many large lavender and rosemary bushes that my mother had planted in the back yard soon after they arrived. The bushes were large enough to drape a wet sheet over to dry, the added benefit being the lovely fragrance that transferred to the fabric. There was no such shrubbery at our farm and I found myself bringing chairs out of the kitchen, leaning tool handles across the chair backs, and all manner of inconvenient measures in order to dry my washing.

One day I was busy in one of the upstairs bedrooms, repairing a torn quilt when I heard digging and hammering. I thought nothing of it for Abram and his men were ever busy with some kind of work. When I went downstairs Abram called me to come to the back yard.

He had put several large posts in the ground about eight feet apart. They were deeply notched about six inches from the top and slender linden tree poles that had been stripped of their bark, went from post to post and were attached with wooden pegs, creating a perfect place to dry laundry.

My first thought was how much work this was going to save. My next thought was of a husband who was so considerate of his wife. But that was not the only instance. On every marketing trip to the Yadkin, Augusta, or Charleston, he returned with some small item for me. It was always just something to have, to enjoy, not something I needed for practical purposes, a pewter candlesnuffer, a small mirror in an ivory frame, or a pair of tiny pearl earrings.

Once I met a lady in Puzzle Creek, a cousin of one of my father's neighbors, who wore a dress of such fabric as I had never seen. I sighed over it, likely more times than I realized, for the next time Abram went to the Yadkin, he returned with an entire bolt, only the color was much prettier, a soft sage green that complimented my auburn hair and green eyes.

Our first child, Nancy, was born in March of seventeen eighty-three, twenty-three months after we were married. Abram and my parents were concerned about the amount of time necessary for a mid-wife to reach our place when I needed her.

It was decided that when I neared my time of confinement, my mother and the mid-wife would come to the farm, the mid-wife leaving after the birth, and my mother staying on for a while. The delivery was easy and uncomplicated and I could see the pride and love in Abram's eyes when he was finally allowed to enter the bedroom to see his daughter.

The next ten years passed rapidly, each a mirror image of the last with few exceptions. Abram was appointed as Magistrate to try civil cases in our county of Rutherford.

Our farming endeavors succeeded beyond our expectations. Abram built a gristmill by a great rushing falls on our creek, and a forge near the barn, the only mill and forge in the area. Soon the road to our farm became well-traveled.

After word spread about the first crop of foals from Abram's blood horses, he had buyers all the way from the Yadkin and up to Pennsylvania on a waiting list for the next spring. And, we were blessed with five more children, two boys and three girls. I foreswore any reservations I had felt upon first seeing our four bedroom cabin.

In ninety-three, we admitted another member to our household. She was the daughter of an unmarried weaver, Lucy Hanks, and was offered to us as a bondservant. The child was small for her age, which was ten years, the same as our Nancy.

Even though she hardly spoke, I could see something in her face, a maturity of sorts, born I suspected from the hardships brought on by her mother's irregular situation. Abram's only condition was that the legalities be preserved with a binding contract that I soon realized was a very wise move.

Nancy Hanks, as her name turned out to be, and our Nancy were soon friends and after a short spell of apprehension, I was pleased to see that she influenced our daughter for the better. She took her responsibilities with the younger children seriously and showed amazing patience with them where our Nancy was wont to be easily perturbed. Nancy Hanks was quickly at my side when I needed help of any kind, and as the months passed, I found no cause to regret our decision. At times I wondered what manner of man her father was, for I could see little similarity to Lucy Hanks, physically or by her nature.

She was an apt pupil at whatever she turned her hand, whether her lessons, housekeeping skills, or caring for the children. Actually, the only way our Nancy outdistanced her was in the social graces, dancing and conversation.

Nancy Hanks was on the reserved side in that regard, possibly because she reminded herself that she was, after all, a servant, a fact the rest of us were wont to forget because of our fondness for her and her value to us.

Another ten years passed, distinguished from each other only by those years when another child was born. Abram never failed to show the same excitement every time he walked in to see a newborn son or daughter. By the time our Nancy was nineteen our family had grown to twelve, five boys, and seven girls, and of course, Nancy Hanks.

Abram was a natural-born schoolteacher; in fact, I suspect if he had never left Charleston, he might have chosen that profession. He was demanding of his students, our children, but had the ability to arouse their curiosity, an emotion necessary to learning in most areas of study.

Both Nancys substituted in the classroom when Abram was gone on trips to markets in Charleston or Augusta, or to Rutherfordton, our county seat, to exercise his magisterial duties. Sometimes, after he returned, both girls were allowed to take a trip to Puzzle Creek where they would stay a few days with the Battles whom I had known since my childhood and whose daughter Sally was the same age as our Nancy.

On one of the girl's trips, the Battles had a visitor, a young cousin named Arthur Thompson, a Moravian who had left his religion and his people and gone to Kentucky with a group of settlers. He acquired a large tract of land and had come through Rutherford to visit the Battles on his way back to Kentucky from the Yadkin.

Our Nancy was bemused by him and spoke of scarcely anything else for days after the visit. We tried to discourage her but it was not to be.

Our Nancy had been relatively quiet on the subject of Mr. Thompson for a few weeks and we were lulled into a sense of relief that proved to be false. Again we allowed her and Nancy Hanks to visit the Battle's for a few days.

When a half-day had passed beyond the time they should have been home, we became anxious. By the end of the day we were frantic with worry. Abram rode into Puzzle Creek and finally coaxed a reluctant disclosure from the elder Battle daughter on the whereabouts of the two girls. He returned home in a most dejected state.

For the remainder of the day, he went from frustration and anger to fear for our daughter's safety. He was awake for most of the night and woke me several times as he paced the kitchen floor.

Early the next morning, Nancy Hanks returned and quietly informed us of the events of the past thirty hours. Our Nancy had eloped with Arthur Thompson and they were even now on their way to Kentucky as man and wife.

After bursting into tears fueled by pain and disappointment, I turned my anger on Nancy Hanks. Her patient and quiet explanation was that she accompanied the couple because she wanted to make sure that our Nancy and Mr. Thompson were legally married.

We accepted her account but the disappointment stayed with us for days. Abram took it worse than I because he had always been so close to Nancy.

After a few days had passed, we began to look for a bright side and simply hoped that the young man was as good a fellow as the Battle's believed him to be.

Nancy Hanks

My very first memory is that of the beater pounding against the heddles and the shuttle singing across the warp as my mother went about her weaving. I must have been about four at that time for she had removed me from her brother's house near Puzzle Creek, as she did sporadically, to accompany her as she went from farm to farm weaving flax, wool or cotton into whatever manner of cloth her temporary employer desired. My trips with her were never very lengthy and by the time I was six she had ceased the practice altogether.

So I lived with my Uncle Richard and his wife and children, of which there was a houseful. One of the great surprises of my young life was when I learned that one of the children was actually my sister!

Her name was Amanda but she was called Mandy. We were completely opposite in looks, she being fair haired, blue eyed, and short, even for a four year old. When she came to Uncle Richard's, I did not know, for there was constant coming and going in his household.

I never learned if the other children were all his own or if some were like my sister and me, castoffs that he had taken in. He was a kindly man and worked as a shoemaker when he was not incapacitated by drink. He always meant to quit and would hold his wife and all us children to his breast after his bouts with rum and swear never to touch the stuff again.

But in a very short time, he would go missing and maybe a fortnight later would be dumped from a wagon bed to the lane in front of the house. Usually a week was sufficient to return him to some semblance of normalcy, but sometimes he would be ill and feverish from sleeping on the ground and would need additional nursing.

But I loved him in spite of it all for he was never harsh or cruel. Indeed, I pitied him, for all his family had moved to faraway Kentucky and he had no one to look to for help. My mother did not count for she roamed through North Carolina, Virginia and sometimes South Carolina, never staying long in one place.

She did show up once more, though, and after that I was never to see my poor uncle again. His wife put my scant belongings together and my mother and I departed with scarcely time to say goodbye to my sister Mandy, of whom I had grown quite fond.

I was ten years old and had not seen my mother for four years. As usual, she was cool and aloof and ignored my questions about our destination. In a hired cart we passed through the settlement of Puzzle Creek and continued with not a word between us down a well-worn road that quickly left the settlement behind.

After what seemed many hours, probably made so by the silence, we arrived at a large log house that sat at the foot of two mountains. Oddly enough, what first impressed me was the orderliness. All buildings, including the house, were well kept, fences were neatly built with no missing rails, and a garden near a springhouse was lush with neat rows of vegetables like the flower gardens I had seen in Puzzle Creek.

After we stepped down from the cart, I moved toward the house but my mother grabbed my shoulder and steered me toward the barn where a tall man was sharpening an ax on a grindstone being turned by a black man. She spoke to the man and he put down the ax and motioned for us to follow him.

He stopped at the door of the springhouse, went inside and returned with two gourd dippers, one filled with water for my mother, the other with cold milk for me. I looked up at him as I accepted the gourd and I thought he must be the tallest man in the world.

We stood in the shade of a large chestnut tree while he and my mother talked so low that I could understand only a word now and then. He turned abruptly and guided us into the house and to the kitchen where a woman was kneading bread. She covered the dough with a cloth and showed us to a wondrously furnished parlor.

She and my mother talked and I could understand more of their words than I had before. I was frightened at the possibility of what lay before me but not enough to cry and stir my mother's ire, which was terrible indeed when aroused. Soon their conversation ended and my mother left, giving me only a cursory glance on her way out.

I was never to see her again. I would learn later that she had sold me as a bondservant.

The lady, who turned out to be Mrs. Enloe, wife of the tall man, was pleasant looking with auburn hair and green eyes. She was taller than most women but not unnaturally so. She seated me at the kitchen table and gave me a piece of sweetish tasting bread and milk in a pewter cup.

When I had finished, she took me back into the parlor where her six children were gathered. She very firmly told me each of their names and introduced me as Miss Hanks. To my surprise and delight, the eldest, a girl larger than I but who turned out to be less than a year older, was also called Nancy.

I made very little impression on the younger children for they fled the house as soon as their mother allowed, excepting the smallest who could not yet walk. Nancy and I followed her siblings outside, as it was her job to look after and keep them out of trouble.

Later in the day, Mrs. Enloe explained in detail to me as though I was an adult that my mother had bound me over to them. She went on to say that she hoped I would be happy living with her family. I thought it generous of her to express a sentiment of that kind since I was now a servant and did not warrant such consideration.

Two objectives were settled at the supper table that evening, where I was surprised and pleased to find myself seated beside Nancy. Since our names were the same, Mr. and Mrs. Enloe had decided that their daughter would be called just Nancy, while I would answer to my full name, Nancy Hanks. One of the boys began to repeat my name very rapidly, giggling at the sound of it. Mrs. Enloe threatened to send him away without his supper if he did not stop. I was surprised that she did not need to raise her voice but when I saw him sneak a look at his father I could see why.

Mr. Enloe's face, which I had not noticed before, was dark and angular, his hair raven black, and he looked out from under shaggy black brows with the most extraordinary eyes I had ever seen. He barely scowled but there was no doubt that his son understood for he quitted immediately.

The second point depended on Nancy, or so it seemed, for her parents asked her where she thought I should sleep. I had never heard an adult ask the advice of a child, so I held my breath to see if it would be followed. Nancy spoke immediately and emphatically.

"In my room, of course, Papa. Where else?"

From that day forward, I loved her as I might love a dear sister and indeed, she treated me as such.

In the following months, I was to begin learning many skills that would remain with me for the rest of my life. Helping Nancy with the children was very little different from what I had done at Uncle Richard's.

But, in addition, I performed many small jobs for Mrs. Enloe that she very kindly said lessened her household burdens. It became my job to keep up with her sewing basket so I could fetch it quickly anytime she had a moment to sit down. She depended on me, always and without being told, to bring milk and butter from the springhouse for each meal.

I snapped beans, peeled potatoes and cored apples, which freed Mrs. Enloe to give her attention to the meat and bread of the meal, of which Mr. Enloe was very fond. I learned to prepare pumpkins, beans, and apples for drying and how to make a perfect loaf of potato bread.

Mrs. Enloe made lye soap each fall after hog killing. First the hog fat would be rendered for use in cooking and the remains would be rendered again for soap. George and Moses were instructed to burn hickory wood in their fireplace and save the fine white ashes through which water would be leached to make lye. Water, lye, and fat were combined in a large kettle and cooked over an outdoor fire.

At first the odor was foul but with proper stirring soon turned into a fine, creamy clean smelling soap. There was no drudgery in doing laundry with such good soap, especially when the Enloe's had the only clothes drying poles I had ever seen.

I learned to sew and mend my own clothing. Mrs. Enloe was generous with cloth and I always had several working dresses and a nicer one for Sunday.

Nancy was a bit of a gamine and very rough on her clothing. A sadly torn dress would be passed on to me and with the skills I had acquired, could be made to look almost new. If Nancy did not like the color or pattern of a particular gown, she would be intentionally rowdy because she knew the annoyance caused by a damaged garment was softened by its transferal to me, therefore not being wasted.

However, all was not work. The next week after my arrival, Mr. Enloe included me in his children's already well-organized education. At my uncle's I had learned to read a little and write my own name and a few other words and phrases.

After a few months, I had nearly caught up with Nancy. We read excerpts from many books that Mr. Enloe owned, very little of which I understood in the beginning. I came to like the poetry of Mr. Ladd, whose works had been sent to Mr. Enloe by his Charleston family, and Arthur Lawson's *History of North_Carolina*, especially where he told an amusing story of the Indians who thought they would sell their furs directly to the British instead of the colonists and therefore set sail for England in their canoes, and his description of a ghost ship that was frequently seen on the Carolina coast and was thought to be that of Sir Walter Raleigh.

I did not care for William Byrd's history in which he depicted all North Carolina men as wretches, louts, and sluggards. As I matured, I came to find much of interest in Jefferson's *Notes on the State of Virginia,* which Nancy could not understand, her preference being for much lighter fare.

I read any part of the Bible that was assigned to us but my favorite was Psalms in which I found a quiet pleasure.

Even the Sundays when the Enloe's did not attend church, we were expected to behave in a quiet and respectful manner. When we attended, even stricter rules applied.

Occasionally after church, many of the congregation would gather in one home and spend the afternoon eating, swapping stories and catching up on the latest news from the Yadkin and Watauga settlements. I met other girls of my own age and became acquainted with a few of them but Nancy Enloe remained my best friend and spilled her heart to me on any and all subjects without reservation.

From time to time I thought of my sister Mandy and wondered if she was still at Uncle Richard's or if my mother had seen fit to take her away. It was only by chance that I overheard a comment in Puzzle Creek one day about how fortunate the Pratt family was to have a young bondservant named Mandy Hanks.

Apparently she had inherited our mother's talent and had become an accomplished carder, spinner, and weaver.

The saddest time in all my young years with the Enloe's came when a visitor from Rutherfordton brought news that Uncle Richard had burned to death in his home at Belmont while his wife and children were away visiting relatives. I knew few would mourn him but I remembered only a naturally kind man who was always repentant of his actions but had not the will to overcome them.

Except for my sister Mandy, he was my only relative of whom I was aware and for days I felt very alone. But, grief cannot last forever and after a while I was able to accept his death. However, acceptance did not keep me from waking up in the night in a cold terror, having dreamt of him screaming for me to pull him from the flames.

Except for church, our social occasions were few. Now and then, during the summer, a family in Puzzle Creek would organize a gathering of young people with music and dancing. Nancy and I attended these functions only seldom before age sixteen, but afterwards, nearly always.

She was bright and never shied from conversation or dancing. I was shy with strangers, terribly self-conscious about dancing and therefore attended as more spectator than participant, much to Nancy's chagrin, for she wanted us to be always doing the same thing.

I was more comfortable at home where Nancy and I shared an interest in most areas, including her father's horses. He had brought several from Virginia that were lately of England. They were tall, but strong and healthy riding stock for which there was beginning to be a great demand in the area. Mr. Enloe treated his horses with a deference that some men did not show even to their families. He and Nancy spoke of the bloodlines of Bajazett, Bay Bolton, Dodsworth, and Layton March as though they were discussing kings and queens.

She was first to be informed when a new foal appeared. Mrs. Enloe was a bit concerned at Nancy's interest in horses, an area she felt was not quite proper for a young lady. As usual, Nancy ignored her mother and insisted that I continue to accompany her to the pasture to feed the mares and their offspring the precious carrots that she filched from the cellar.

However, when Nancy had just passed her nineteenth birthday, an occasion arose where she was hardly aware of my existence. Mr. Enloe had magisterial business in Gilbert Town that had been our county seat until Rutherfordton replaced it in 1787.

Mrs. Enloe decided that she would accompany him on his trip. Nancy and I were to care for the younger children, who were reduced to nine, for the two eldest sons, Joseph and William, were now in school in Charleston and staying with Mr. Enloe's family. We were to continue their lessons just as Mr. Enloe taught them, and we did.

The Enloe's arrived home on Thursday to find everything in a very orderly state and in way of reward, allowed us a trip to Puzzle Creek to visit with the Battle family whose daughter Sally was our age.

The next day, when we put our small hand baggage into the wagon, we had no idea that this visit would change our lives forever.

Arthur Thompson was twenty-three, handsome and well spoken. Within hours of arriving at the Battle's where he was a guest, Nancy was totally infatuated and it was quite obvious that he shared her feelings.

During our five-day visit, they were seldom out of each other's company, although, to her credit, Nancy was very discreet and Mr. Thompson certainly observed the proprieties. On our way home she could talk of nothing else and she was not reticent when she spoke of him to her parents. I could see the concern on their faces and wished that I could tell them that this was just another of Nancy's whimsical ideas, like when she decided that she would like to make her own way in the world as a horse breeder.

Not until her father convinced her of how reviled she would be in such an entirely masculine profession had she backed down and changed her mind. But, she never wavered in her devotion to Mr. Thompson, no matter how her parents tried to dissuade her.

Mr. Enloe went to the Battle's with the distinct purpose of meeting this paragon who had so captured his daughter's affection. He had expected to dislike the young man but came away with a reluctant admiration for his composure and for his excellent reputation with Mr. Battle, for whose opinion Mr. Enloe retained a great respect.

Nevertheless, Mr. and Mrs. Enloe tried to convince Nancy that she was too young and inexperienced to marry and brave the wilds of Kentucky, to which Nancy countered by reminding her mother that she was two years younger when she and Mr. Enloe were married.

The commotion quieted and I believe the Enloe's began to think that Nancy might have lost some of her ardor for Mr. Thompson. Certainly, they felt comfortable allowing us to visit the Battle's once more since he was no longer a guest in their home.

Mr. Enloe drove us to Puzzle Creek and was scarcely out of earshot when Nancy began to disclose the details of a plan for elopement she had worked out with Mr. Thompson at secret meetings that had taken place since our last stay in Puzzle Creek. I was horrified and tried with all my being to discourage her but she was steadfast in her intentions. She swore me to secrecy and as her dear friend I could not betray her trust.

They were to leave Puzzle Creek in the dead of night to avoid involving the Battle family. I was trying to decide how I would ever break the news to the Enloe's when Nancy quite off-handedly mentioned that Mr. Thompson had not been able to get in touch with Reverend Swabel, the minister in a small settlement north of Puzzle Creek, but hoped to find him at home when they arrived.

If not, they still intended to proceed to Kentucky. I was greatly shocked and spoke severely, reminding her of what the consequences would be if she persisted in accompanying a man to whom she was not married on a journey of several days and nights duration.

She listened quietly but would not change her plans, so I changed mine and was as adamant as she. I slipped out of the house with her that night just after ten o'clock. Mr. Thompson awaited us with a wagon at the northern edge of the settlement. His surprise at seeing me was obvious but I could also sense that he was not wholly at ease with the entire situation.

We rode quietly and reached Duncan's Creek at daybreak to find Reverend Swabel just arising. They were married within the hour and left for Kentucky after a long and tearful parting between Nancy and me, of which Mr. Thompson was very understanding. Reverend Swabel arranged for a neighbor to drive me back to the Enloe's.

Mr. Enloe had just gotten back from Puzzle Creek where he had learned from Sally Battle, who had apparently overheard part of our conversation, that Nancy and Arthur Thompson planned to elope. Since she could give no details about where they intended to go, Mr. Enloe had not tried to pursue them.

It was with a heavy heart that I entered the Enloe home to give them the details of Nancy's elopement. Mr. Enloe was plainly hurt and disappointed but seemed to appreciate my efforts to make sure his daughter was indeed married before leaving for Kentucky.

Mrs. Enloe became very angry and began to rebuke me harshly for not finding a way to deter Nancy from her plan. I did not argue with her and at last her anger waned. She acknowledged that I had likely done my best, considering Nancy's headstrong nature and she expressed her appreciation to me for accompanying the couple to Duncan's Creek.

After a few days, everything was almost back to normal but I could still see the distress in Mr. Enloe's face and I knew he missed her for he began to seek me out for the same kind of conversations that he had so enjoyed with his Nancy.

I, also, missed Nancy terribly, and was filled with a restlessness that I had never known before. I knew that I had less than two years left of my bondservant contract but had no idea of what I would do when that date arrived.

If my life with the Enloe's had been a regrettable one, I would have been counting the weeks until I was free. As it was, I dreaded the day when I would have to leave this family and make my way in a world where I had few friends and no kin that I could go to.

The postal rider left mail at Mr. Battle's store every Tuesday or Wednesday so I convinced Mrs. Enloe to let me ride one of Mr. Enloe's gentle mares to Puzzle Creek each Thursday to see if Nancy had written. On my return, Mrs. Enloe would be standing in the door watching my face to see if there was any news.

Many trips occurred before I had reason to rejoice. I began singing loudly before I reached the house and when I was where I could see Mrs. Enloe, I waved the letter over my head and she came running to meet me.

Harrodsburg, Kentucky
2 October 1802

My Dear Father and Mother,

It is with great trepidation that I write to you so soon after engaging in an action that I am certain met with your strongest disapproval. However, now that it is done, and irrevocable, allow me to assure you both that I have no cause to regret our elopement, nor do I believe I ever will have. Mr. Thompson has a naturally kind and generous nature and treats me with great affection and respect. Until our cabin is built, we are to stay with his friends, the Andrews, a congenial couple of not more than five years our senior, who warmly received us upon our arrival. They have two sons, ages three and five, who remind me of my brothers at that age.

Most importantly, let me assure you that Mr. Thompson did not coerce me in any way to elope. Indeed, quite the opposite. It was altogether through my persuasion that he eventually agreed to make our arrangements, the whole affair going against his sense of honor.

Now that you have been assured of my comfort and safety, and indeed, my happiness, may I beg a promise from you? My dear parents, please do not attach any culpability to Nancy Hanks for my conduct. Yes, she accompanied us to Duncan's Creek, but only to prevent me from committing an act of recklessness should the minister not be available. Be assured, if that had been the case, Nancy Hanks would have prevailed and brought me back home directly.

I am sure that when we have your permission to visit, Mr. Thompson will endeavor by every instance in his power to merit your regard and express his gratitude to two persons whom his affectionate wife loves very dearly.

If you do not object to hearing from me again, in my next letter I will describe the beauty and richness of the countryside here around Harrodsburg.

I am, with great fondness, your most loving daughter,

Nancy Enloe Thompson.

Chapter Two

Abram Enloe

Our Nancy was barely settled in Kentucky and I was already overcome with a terrible restlessness. I missed her most keenly for we shared an interest in many areas and spent a good deal of time in conversation, particularly about our horses. She was a lively and intelligent child and had maintained those attributes as a young woman, along with a slight streak of stubbornness.

Her mother did not hesitate to tell me that I spoiled our Nancy by encouraging her interests in areas not considered quite seemly for a young woman. I could see that Sarah was on the verge of openly blaming me when Nancy eloped with Arthur Thompson.

But she managed to hold her tongue, and well she did for we had had many discussions over the years about how harsh words, although they may be forgiven, can never truly be forgotten, for they hang suspended above us ready to drop into the slightest quarrel.

Well, our Nancy was gone and I found myself envying her move. I treasured what we had built here in Rutherford but I missed the challenge of the wilderness. And we were decidedly no longer a wilderness for the population of the county had grown and there were many settlers west of us where there had been none when I arrived in 1780.

A few years before, a friend and frontiersman had obtained and passed on to me a copy of Arthur Filson's book on the settlement of Kentucky that also contained the adventures of Daniel Boone. Filson's prose was somewhat flowery for me but I did not question a single story that Boone told of his wilderness adventures.

I had heard a constant stream of these stories in the Charleston warehouses all during my youth and had been fascinated with Boone's love of the wilderness and his exploits. I had never forgotten my disappointment at having barely missed him in 1779 when I first came to the Yadkin from Charleston.

The tales recounted in Filson's book rang true and I had passed many a cold winter evening reading it by the fire. Perhaps recollections of Boone were what spurred me on in my thoughts of moving west, although I knew already it would not be beyond the Blue Ridge.

I had heard talk in Puzzle Creek and at the markets of many people moving, passing through the Cumberland Gap and into Kentucky, on to the Ohio

Valley and even beyond. In my estimation, this was folly when, by many accounts, fine land was available southwest of Asheville, a small town that lay in a wide valley in Buncombe County.

Of course, in the back of my mind I also knew that where Sarah might be convinced to move west in North Carolina, she would never be so persuaded to go to Kentucky.

I daresay I thought overmuch on the subject for Sarah resolutely scolded me one day for forgetting a bolt of huckaback, a coarse linen toweling that the store in Puzzle Creek had ordered for her. We had long passed the time when we hired itinerant weavers like Lucy Hanks to weave our cloth, it being cheaper and more convenient to order it ready made.

Perhaps missing our Nancy and Sarah's unusual sharpness together with my having just turned forty-three and again struck with wanderlust came together to point me in the direction of an event that was to drastically influence the remainder of our lives.

April had arrived after an unusually cold March and I knew that Sarah would soon be getting anxious to visit family and friends in Puzzle Creek. Our only wagon comfortable for travel had returned from its last trip with a split tongue and had not yet been repaired. Not finding the necessary tools to start work, I looked for Moses but he was nowhere to be found.

"Moses, where are you hiding, you rascal?"

No answer. I knew I might as well find what I needed for the old man was likely already sitting on the creek bank swatting flies and casting his hook in hopes of a fat trout for his supper.

The April sun was warm and I removed my coat and hung it on the handle of a plow that sat outside the barn awaiting the spring fields. The cool shade of the barn was pleasant but as I turned the hall corner, I saw that I was not alone.

Nancy Hanks was descending the loft, an egg basket in the crook of her arm, and one hand holding up her skirt, the other grasping each rung of the ladder as she carefully stepped down. Each movement revealed a well-turned ankle above a small foot.

I don't believe she was aware of my approach. As I drew near, her foot slipped off the second to last rung and eggs went flying in all directions. I was close enough to catch her before she could fall.

My long arms seemed to move of their own accord and wrap around her. I held her against me and whirled her around and around as though we were dancing, although her feet never touched the floor.

Her slim but sturdy shoulders were caught in my embrace and I seemed unable to release her. She trembled slightly, tilted her head and looked directly into my eyes, an honest, straightforward look that seemed to ask, "What does this mean?"

Only the faint color in her cheeks and the pulse that throbbed at the base of her throat betrayed her emotions.

"Nancy…Nancy…"

Unwillingly I relaxed my arms and let her feet slip to the floor. She took a step back, looked at me once more, and fled the barn, the empty egg basket clutched against her breast.

Only then did I realize that never a word had passed between us. Even her name had sounded only in my head and now a thousand other thoughts and visions and feelings were swimming there too, making me feel as though I was still whirling her around in my arms.

Never a day's peace came to me after that. Nancy Hanks was in my mind every waking moment and in my dreams at night. I had seen her on a daily basis for over ten years but had never looked at her except the way I would look at any well-turned lass at a community gathering or when I rode to the markets.

Now I noticed her every movement about the house. Where she had been just another member of our household, now she seemed to be everywhere my eyes turned.

She never looked back at me but now and then I caught a fleeting glance when she thought I was not looking in her direction. I tried to tell myself that nothing of consequence had taken place. Why, I had not even spoken but had simply caught the girl to prevent her from falling.

Then it would all come rushing back, that sensation when she was in my arms. My head would whirl and I would be almost dizzy from remembering. Nancy...Nancy.

I tried to avoid her without being obvious to Sarah, but it was difficult. When Nancy Hanks found it necessary to speak to me, she was almost stone faced; nevertheless I could see something in her eyes that had not been there before.

Before too many days passed, I was fortunate to receive a visit from Felix Walker who had given me Filson's book on Boone many years before. We had become the best of friends and were of like mind on the subject of moving farther west in North Carolina as opposed to west beyond the mountains. He aspired to be a congressman and thereby was required to own at least three hundred acres of land.

After the Revolution all North Carolina taxpayers were permitted to vote so it was in any politicians best interests to better the economic status of those residents in his constituency.

Also, Walker knew the ins and outs of procuring and filing for land to avoid the pitfalls of the infamous Transylvania Company that had been created by Richard Henderson and Daniel Boone. The how and whys of the company's failure were complex, no doubt, but it seemed that much was taken for granted when it came to filing proper claims.

We would not do so, for we intended to secure a legitimate title to whatever property we acquired before we made a move.

There, I had said it. I believe at that moment I intended to go west at all costs. Walker had to leave but we made plans for a five-day hunting trip the next week.

I kept myself fully occupied around the farm for the next week, having as little to do with Nancy Hanks as possible as much to avoid distressing her as to avoid arousing Sarah's suspicions. Nancy did not exactly avoid me but she seemed to hardly ever be in the same room as I. We had to pass near each other in the kitchen one morning and I sensed, rather than felt, her body go rigid as I went by.

I tried often to convince myself that our small encounter was just that, a minute instance that would fade away as time passed. But her face remained in my mind, as did the warmth of her body in my arms. Those few seconds when I pressed her against me continued to feel more real than anything I had ever experienced.

Her face told me that she felt the same way. Deep in my heart I knew the truth. I was bewitched and impassioned by this girl who was half my age and who lived in my home as a bondservant although we had long regarded her as a member of our family.

The day I was to meet Felix Walker arrived and I left before daylight, saying goodbye to Sarah while she still lay beneath her bedcovers. I looked forward to the possibility that the trip would help me to turn my thoughts from Nancy Hanks.

Felix awaited me at the edge of a meadow on his property with the news that our trip would be cut short by two days because he intended to travel to Raleigh, our state capitol, to witness a special session that had been hastily called to vote on a resolution commending Thomas Jefferson for his success in the purchase of the Louisiana Territory. Jefferson was more farmer than politician and was very well thought of in our area.

The hunt took us deep into the forest and although our hounds scented and pursued several deer, by the middle of the second day we had not fired a single shot except at rabbits that we cooked for our meals. We turned back but darkness had fallen by the time we reached Felix's house. He insisted I stay the night for although wild animals had become scarce in our area, a panther or bear could do serious injury or worse to a lone traveler.

Over beakers of applejack we talked of the western lands and agreed to meet again to plan a scouting trip to the area. As we rose to retire, Felix asked if something else was on my mind.

He seemed to think that I was distracted all through our hunt and during our evening conversation. I emphatically assured him not, hoping he would believe my falsehood.

The next morning I was on the road as soon as a faint light showed from the east. Four hours later I rode into my own yard with a sense of dread. What could I do to rid myself of this all-consuming obsession? I knew I must conquer it, for not to do so was to invite disaster.

The aroma of baking bread greeted me as I entered an unusually quiet house. Calling to Sarah, I entered the kitchen to find instead Nancy Hanks removing loaves of potato bread from the hearth, her cheeks rosy from the heat.

Her surprise was obvious and she hesitantly explained that Sarah had taken the older children with her to Puzzle Creek, leaving only Jane and Essie who were asleep upstairs. Nancy Hanks did not look at me as she spoke.

When I stepped close and laid my hands on her shoulders, my conscious intention was to allay her disquiet, but only later would I remember a quote from some long forgotten essay or sermon about the road to perdition being paved with good intentions.

She yielded to me with a trust that made me ashamed, but not so much so that I reversed my direction. When our passion was spent, and I truly believed that her pleasure was equal to mine, we lay without speaking. Even in our silence there was a sweet intimacy and no need for words.

As the days passed, I searched my soul for the strength to overcome this obsession that had taken over my being, but with no success. One problem was that I could not convince myself that my feelings for Nancy Hanks were wrong, or at least, of a sordid nature.

And, if I had even the slightest conception that she did not return my affection in full, I believe I might have been able to stop. As it stood, I continued in a quandary and sought to dull the ache by working harder than I had done in many years.

Sarah seemed puzzled by my manner but she had seen me work out problems in this way before. I suspect she thought I was struggling with some decision about moving, a subject on which we had spoken very little so far.

Nancy Hanks and I reverted to our former behavior of pretending not to be aware of each other's existence. Miraculously, Sarah did not notice. Three weeks later, Felix Walker returned from Raleigh and armed with maps, we rode west to look for land.

Our trip took us through places that not many white men's feet had trod. When we reached the region beyond the French Broad River, we knew we were heading in the right direction.

Forests of gigantic trees stretched as far as the eye could see in every direction. Streams were plentiful and rushed from the hollows creating waterfalls around every bend that stunned the eye with their majesty and the ear with their roar.

We passed a bald mountain, higher in altitude, but not unlike the one where we had defeated Ferguson and his British troops twenty-three years before. On one of the maps that had been made for my companion, the bald was called the "Tanasee," obviously an Indian name.

We rode to the top and cooked our midday meal while enjoying a glorious view of the surrounding mountains.

Finally we reached the area where we hoped to buy land and were almost overcome by the richness of every aspect, water, soil, timber and wildlife. The area I was to purchase lay just east of a high dome shaped mountain of great height.

A note on the map said the Cherokee Indians called the area the Ocona Lufta. I liked the sound of the name, the way it rolled off my tongue like a waterfall. I chose a site for our home a few miles east of the mountain that was not unlike the one in Rutherford, near water and fuel, with natural meadows not too far away.

The site was already level enough for building so I carried stones and stacked them at the corners of what would encompass the foundation of our new house. Then I blazed several trees around the site and cut my initials into one so there would be no question of ownership.

We spent the better part of two days reaching the area where Felix wanted to locate. His land was east by northeast, and like mine, was towered over by a gigantic mountain but circling this one were great stone tors that sat precipitously around its crest.

Although reluctant to leave the peace of the wilderness, we both knew we must. May was half over and there was ahead of us literally weeks of constant work in preparing for the move.

Felix was to take care of purchasing the sections of land from a veteran who had received them for his contribution to the war. And of course, he would make sure all the necessary paperwork was filed to avoid the many pitfalls that could come about because so much land changed hands so frequently.

Our trip home took less time but was not so enjoyable for we forced ourselves to travel at a brisk pace and did not stop to marvel at the glorious nature around us.

We reached Felix's house at dusk and retired early. I left before sunrise the next morning and hurried home to convince Sarah that this move would be a fine adventure. I arrived to find her unfit to discuss anything of a serious nature and without her faithful Nancy Hanks.

Sarah's only illnesses over the years had grown from simple colds that seemed to settle in her throat. When this happened, the only cure was to lie abed and sip her honey and whiskey remedy until she was better. She was hoarse and feverish and inquired hardly at all about my trip but instructed me to drive directly to Duncan's Creek and bring Nancy Hanks home.

Sarah had given her leave to visit a friend, Polly Price, and had taken sick two days later. I must admit that my heart sank a bit when thirteen-year-old Mary begged to go with me. Before I could speak her mother shushed her, reminding her that she needed to prepare vegetables for our supper.

On the two hour drive to Duncan's Creek I tried to think only of Sarah and the coming move but a tiny speck of anticipation at seeing Nancy Hanks had grown almost to a fury by the time I arrived at the Price's. She did not even look at me until we were in the wagon and heading for home.

Then, she tried to speak, but instead began to sob. I drove the wagon off the road into a grove of white pines. My attempt at consolation soon turned into another episode of passion on a thick carpet of pine needles that lay in the shade of the gigantic trees.

Afterwards, we talked and I attempted to make her understand that I loved her but that I still loved Sarah and could never leave her. I went around and around in circles and always ended up at the same juncture.

On the seat beside me as we drove home, Nancy Hanks spoke for the first time, quietly and unambiguously, and my opinion of her was greater than before. I believe she did understand but still I felt the fool for my inability to resolve the situation.

Any action I considered taking was likely to raise Sarah's suspicions. I was caught in a grim trap of my own making with no way to pry open the jaws.

Sarah was pleased to see Nancy Hanks and the children thronged around her as if she had been gone for months. I had just left the parlor where Sarah lay on a daybed when her words chilled my heart.

"Nancy Hanks! How on earth did you soil the back of your good dress?"

Nancy's voice came calmly in her usual quiet and composed manner.

"Polly and I climbed the hill behind her house this morning and on our way back down I lost my footing and fell."

"Well," said Sarah, "thank goodness you didn't turn an ankle!"

I breathed a sigh of relief and left the house scorning myself for the deception but warmed by the memory of how Nancy Hanks had felt in my arms.

Two days passed before I broached a serious discussion of moving with Sarah. She did not attempt to hide her feelings. She thought it unnecessary and made it clear that, in her opinion, the move was all based on a childish desire for adventure.

"But," she said, "if we're moving, and it's plain that you've already made up your mind, the first condition I have is that you have a cabin ready to move into by the time we arrive. I'll sleep in a wagon on the trip because there's no other choice, but not after we get there!"

Since I had expected more resistance from her, I was elated with her response and agreed that the entire process would be decidedly improved if our new cabin greeted us upon arrival. She said very little else except to ask if I knew what other families from the area would be moving with us. I could only speculate on that point because I did not have a definite commitment from anyone except Felix Walker.

My first act was to have my foreman, William Gwynn, round up three young men who would set out to the new land with him in a few days and have a cabin as finished as possible by the time we arrived. I could do no less for Sarah.

I drew up plans and went over them with William. They would build roughly the same structure in which we now lived but at Sarah's insistence, with one bedroom on the ground level in addition to the four upstairs.

I thought her reference to our "not getting any younger" was uncalled for but I intended to keep the peace at all costs. A barn and other outbuildings on the new land would wait until the rest of us arrived.

Felix wrote to say that the land had been purchased and deeds had been filed without a hitch and he would be back in Rutherford in a few days to begin his own arrangements for the journey.

Made easy by the knowledge that our land was secure, we loaded a wagon with all the building tools William's crew would need and other supplies for cooking and sleeping. They would take the wagon trail through Asheville and since their load was lighter than ours would be, we hitched my two draft horses to the wagon.

We loaded corn and oats, and I extracted a promise from William that he would care for them diligently. Oxen would pull our wagons because they were less excitable, stronger and easier to feed on a rough extended journey.

My days were now filled with planning and re-planning all aspects of our move. When Felix arrived, a young fellow accompanied him. He was from the Yadkin and aspired to the political life and had attached himself to Felix to learn the trade, so to speak.

After welcoming Felix and being introduced to young Samuel Horton, Sarah left us alone in the parlor. Our conversations went from the Easterners who valued the western edge of our state for little else than a buffer against possible Indian attack, to what sorry conditions our roads were in, to the high number of distilleries that remained in our area even though there was no blockade of rum from the British as there had been during the war.

Another bee in our bonnets was the lack of markets for the great variety of goods that our region was capable of producing. Virginia had been very tightfisted about allowing North Carolina goods to pass through its state. We had no seaports to speak of and, indeed, even if we had, Charleston was much nearer to the mountains than our own coastline.

Our young guest was waxing almost poetically about the rise in cotton production since Whitney invented his gin, when Nancy Hanks entered the room carrying a tray with a jug of cider and three pewter beakers.

Horton stopped in mid-sentence and rose, almost upsetting the tea table in front of where we sat. He bowed in a most exaggerated manner and offered to take the tray. Nancy quietly put it down, poured each beaker half-full and started to leave the room. Horton scrambled to reach the door first, held it open and again performed his exaggerated bow.

Nancy acknowledged his actions with a barely discernible nod but did not speak. Horton never took his eyes off her and as soon as the door was closed, spoke in a very admiring tone.

"Your daughter, Sir?"

That was not the first time we had been asked that question so my answer was the one we had decided upon many years before.

"No, the daughter of a friend. She has lived with us for many years."

Hard though I tried, the young man's manner toward Nancy Hanks spawned a jealousy in me that I had never known before. I hoped to keep my feelings concealed and thought I had until Felix was leaving and asked if his young associate had annoyed me in some way.

"No," I said. "I'm just distracted by Sarah telling me earlier today that she refuses to move without her furniture. That will require at least two extra wagons that I will have to search for."

The next week was a confusion of plans and re-plans and new plans of things that must be carried out. I had decided that it would be folly to attempt driving all our stock on such a long and difficult journey, especially since experienced drovers were scarce and expensive.

So we cut out the best quality cattle, hogs, and horses and drove the rest to markets in the Yadkin where I acquired the two wagons needed for Sarah's precious furniture.

Upon my arrival back at home, I learned that Sarah had taken the three oldest girls, Mary, Lizzie, and Meggie for an overnight visit to her family in Puzzle Creek. She was wise to do so for the closer to the time of our move, the more everyone would be needed for the thousand and one jobs that must be done before the first wagon rolled.

Nancy Hanks served our supper in near silence, noticed only by me because the young ones were filled with questions about the move. Would we cook on campfires and sleep on the ground and what about wild panthers and bears and Indians and wolves and would any of their friends be moving with us? Nancy never looked at me even after she sat down.

After supper, I waited in the parlor until all the children were in bed, the last question answered and the last goodnight said. Then I spoke softly to Nancy Hanks and walked out to the barn.

The night air was warm and humid but a refreshing breeze came from the west. I waited for her and guided her to a fresh pile of hay.

Afterwards, I lay back and hated myself for not having the courage to end this situation that could not go on indefinitely without discovery. Nancy scolded me gently for being too tough on myself and, in my weakness, I willingly allowed her to do so. Still, I knew in my heart and soul that it would end someday and with no good to anyone.

The next day we began to pack our first wagon with farming and blacksmithing equipment, and whatever carpentry tools William Gwynn had not taken with him. We packed and unpacked and packed again, seeking to fill even the smallest spaces with items that would be difficult to come by in our new wilderness.

One wagon would hold food for us and for the stock. The oxen would need extra food for the energy required to pull the heavy wagons in the kind of places we would travel after leaving Asheville.

The cattle and horses would likely find grazing along the way but would be fed a small ration of oats in the mornings. There was whole corn for the hogs, especially one enormous sow who would be their leader if we kept her well-fed.

Finally the pandemonium slowed and things began to fall into place. The final count of families who would move with us was eight, including Felix Walker. Sarah was happy that the eldest Battle son and his new wife were among the count for that meant that others of this family that she had known all her life might follow later.

Also going along were the Kennedys, Stoakleys, Plotts, Harmanns, Hollifields, and the Wallaces. The Wallaces were Scots-Irish and the least amiable of all our neighbors but if they could muster what they needed, we had no objection to their being a part of our train.

We began to pack the household goods a little at a time and finally were down to just our beds and a few pots and pans. The Welsh cupboard that had been built especially for the house was much too large to fit in a wagon and it looked lonely without the blue dishes that had graced its shelf for so many years.

Sarah had finally agreed to leave the cupboard after I said in frustration, "Would you be wanting me to dismantle the entire house and haul it along?"

She said, "Don't tempt me!" and then remembered that we had made no arrangements for her chickens. I knew it was useless to say that we might get replacements later on so I set Moses to making a large hickory slat basket that could be hung on the side of one of the wagons.

When we stopped for the night the basket could be opened and turned upside down over the chickens so they could be fed and watered and allowed to scratch in the dirt until morning. I could tell by Sarah's smile that she was pleased but she was still disgruntled enough about the move not to be overly generous with her praise.

Moses and George, at my bidding, left their furniture and packed only cooking utensils and gardening tools. George's beehives took much space in one of the wagons but he would not willingly leave them behind.

Also, I knew that Sarah depended on the honey, for real sugar was scarce and expensive and would be even more so in our new wilderness.

Amidst the clamor, Nancy Hanks worked diligently but was mostly silent except with the children. I saw Sarah watching her a few times with a puzzled look. When Nancy and I came close to each other, which it was impossible not to do sometimes, I tried to keep from doing anything to cause her any discomfort.

The day before we were due to leave, Sarah said, "If Joseph and William were here, they could have been a lot of help. I wonder what they'll think of the move?"

"They'd be all for it," I said. "But, we agreed that their education not be interrupted."

Silently my mind was saying that I dreaded the thought of my two son's reactions at finding out about Nancy Hanks and me more than anyone except Sarah. What I was doing went against everything I had taught them of honesty and constancy and honor.

The thought made the trip more welcoming, for ahead would be the trail, the mountaintops and gorges, the danger, the excitement and the physical challenges. Maybe it would be enough to take my thoughts away from the dilemma, at least temporarily.

Finally the morning came when our last few possessions were loaded on the wagons and there was no more to be done. We prepared to bid farewell to a place that we all loved, the place where all our children had been born, the only home Sarah and I had ever known except those in which we spent our childhoods.

Sarah asked me one last time whether I was sure that the Fords, to whom we had leased our house and land, could be trusted to take care of it properly. I assured her that by all accounts they were reliable, industrious people and that several neighbors, including one of her brothers, had promised to happen by now and then to see that all was as it should be.

All at once it was time to go. I tied my five brood mares to the back of the wagons because they were too valuable to move with the loose stock.   I could not look at Sarah, nor could I look at Nancy Hanks so I mounted my horse and rode ahead of the lead wagon.

I could hear the cowbells as we began moving, very slowly at first. Then we picked up to a steady pace and by the time we rounded the last bend, could see our home no more.

<u>Sarah Enloe</u>

Abram started changing from the first moment we learned that our Nancy was gone. I had never seen a man so struck. It was a full ten minutes before he could speak and then it was in the tone of someone totally bewildered.

Nancy's letter helped to ease my mind but Abram continued to cluck like an old mother hen about all manner of evils that might befall her in the wilds of Kentucky. Clearly, he did not recognize her likeness to him.

I think, though, he missed her mostly where the horses were concerned. From early days, they shared a vast knowledge of bloodlines and all manner of what went into the makeup of a good horse.

Our Nancy, according to her father, could recognize the quality of a newborn foal as soon as its feet hit the ground. Over the years she had spent much more time with her father than with me for they also shared the classroom.

I did not feel cheated, even though she was my oldest daughter. After Nancy came Joseph and William, then Mary, Elizabeth, which was shortened to Lizzie, and Margaret, who became Meggie, then Samuel and James, and after that, Jane and Esther, whom we called Essie.

So having one daughter who preferred her father's company was hardly a dilemma. After our Nancy left, Nancy Hanks assumed her responsibilities in the classroom and carried them out very well. She was of a much more studious nature and had ten times our Nancy's patience with the children.

I had never regretted our decision to take her into our home but somehow I had never gotten to know her the way our Nancy had. She had a naturally reserved manner that discouraged personal enquiries even when she seemed in distress, which did not often occur.

Usually she moved about her work with a quiet confidence and that was why I was so startled one day when she burst into the back door of the kitchen. Her face was flushed and she grasped an egg basket to her breast.

"Gracious, Nancy Hanks," I said, "what's the matter?"

She swallowed hard and struggled to speak.

"I...I dropped the basket. All the eggs are broken."

She stood as if awaiting my reproach but I patted her shoulder and said, "Child, don't take on so. We can live with the loss of a few eggs!"

She breathed what seemed a grateful sigh, set the basket on the table and went on her way. I knew that she missed our Nancy, maybe as much as the rest of the family.

Well, she would just have to deal with her loss as we had. I hadn't thought of it lately but her bond would be up in less than two years. I wondered if she had considered her future. Probably not, for she seemed almost oblivious to anything outside her present position.

Life stayed quiet for a while and then one day Abram came home from Puzzle Creek full of stories about a number of families who planned to move to Kentucky or to the Ohio Valley in search of new land. There was a sparkle in his eyes that had not been there when he left that morning.

I watched him as I used to do when we were first married, his large hands moving almost as an extension of his voice. He looked very little older than when we first met, the main difference being the sprinkling of gray at his temples, made very conspicuous by their place amidst his coal black hair.

It seemed odd to think of him being past forty but it mattered little to him for he worked and lived the same as when he was twenty-five. He was still speaking about the movers when I remembered I had asked him to bring home a bolt of huckaback, a coarse toweling material that Mr. Battle had ordered for me.

A bit discomfited at my interruption, he said, "Sarah, I forgot, I just forgot, what with all the talk of new lands and Kentucky. I'll pick it up next week."

"I needed it now, Abram, not next week!"

I know my voice was unusually sharp, for I saw a look on his face that I had seldom seen in all our years together. But, his keen enthusiasm at the talk of moving seemed to grate a bit on my nerves although I was not to understand why for several more days.

Felix Walker had become our friend after he put Abram forth as a candidate for magistrate in our county. I knew Felix's wife Phoebe on a casual basis but he and Abram became personal friends very quickly for they shared many interests outside of politics. Both especially loved hunting with their dogs, a particular mountain breed called Plott hounds. And Felix was first to acquire one of Abram's young blood horses.

When Felix came for a visit, just like Abram, he was full to running over with news about the movers, many of whom had not secured property but were uprooting their families simply on the possibility that they would find land when they arrived in Kentucky.

He recounted the story of the Transylvania Company and how, after putting years of work into cutting trails into the wilderness, Daniel Boone had lost the two thousand acres he had been promised by Judge Richard Henderson, the head of the company. Boone had not legalized the matter and so had no way to contest the loss when the company was dissolved.

I seldom interjected my opinions into the men's discussions but this time I felt duty-bound.

"If this could happen to Daniel Boone, your hero and my father's, it could easily happen to anyone. Shouldn't they be warned? Think of the children among them."

At my behest, both Felix and Abram agreed to speak to the movers before they left for Kentucky.

Then they began to plan a five-day hunting trip for which I was immensely grateful for Abram had begun to wear on my nerves with his unusual reticence. I had spoken to him several times lately and been totally unheard until I repeated myself.

I supposed he was thinking of the movers for he brought out a book that Felix had given him many years before and sat up at night re-reading it. Perhaps the hunting trip was just what was needed to bring back his old self.

They left before daybreak one morning and breakfast was barely over for the rest of us when I decided that during their absence would be a good opportunity for a trip to Puzzle Creek. I had been only one time since early spring and my mother was still weak from a fever contracted the previous winter.

I took all our brood with me except the two youngest and planned to stay overnight. The next day was Thursday, baking day, but I knew that Nancy Hanks could manage very well with only a couple of chits like Jane and Essie to look after.

Puzzle Creek had remained a sleepy settlement for a long time but had changed drastically in the past ten years. The village itself had taken on the appearance of a town with a tavern, a bakery, a tin shop and a livery. Only a few of the faces I saw on my way to my parent's house were familiar to me.

Yes, I could almost commiserate with Abram in his concern about the area becoming overcrowded. After taking leave of my parents and other friends the next morning, I must confess that I was very ready to head the wagon toward home.

Our trip was marked only by a disagreement between Mary and Lizzie as to who would first have a dress from a bolt of blue cambric we had purchased at Mr. Battle's store.

Much to our surprise when we reached home in mid-afternoon, Abram was already there, waving from the barn as we drove up. He greeted us warmly but seemed to grow overly disturbed when he explained about the reduction of the hunting trip.

Nancy Hanks had finished the baking the day before and was now busy with preparations for the evening meal. Her two young charges were noisy and energetic and happy to see us. Everything seemed in order and I remember thinking, "What on earth would I do without her?"

In the coming days Abram seemed driven to find employment around the farm. He worked sometimes as though he were on a crusade. I supposed it was all this talk of going west.

Some men, such as my father, were quiet and speculative when they wrestled with a decision. Abram had always worked out his difficulties doing hard physical labor. I did not press him and left him to deal as he chose with whatever was on his mind.

Barely two weeks after the hunting trip, Felix Walker appeared with maps of a vast area in the western part of our state that could be obtained for an astonishingly small price. It was at that moment that I accepted the idea that we would be resettling, although for some time I would only admit it to myself.

Abram and Felix left to explore the new land, carrying behind their saddles the meager rations they would need to survive, mostly flour, salt, and coffee, a small pot and one skillet, two plates, two beakers and two spoons. Although quite capable of supplementing their rations with game, I reckoned they would be aching for bread and potatoes on their return.

Over the years the steady hum of the mill and forge had become a sound as natural as the bird's singing in the forest so the place seemed quiet without the constant ring of Abram's axe or hammer. After a couple of days, I began to notice that Nancy Hanks was quieter than ever and seemed a few times on the brink of tears. I convinced her to go for a visit with a friend of hers who lived in Duncan's Creek.

Polly Price was an amiable young woman whose parents were agreeable enough although not as resourceful as one could wish. Still, they were responsible people and I thought the change of scene might bring Nancy Hanks out of her doldrums.

So we sent her off with orders to enjoy herself. As luck would have it, I woke the very next morning with a bad sore throat that did not respond to my homemade remedy. With eight children in the house and no Nancy Hanks to look to, I realized quickly how much I had come to rely upon her.

Two days passed and my ailment grew worse. I was almost at the point of feeling sorry for myself, something I was never wont to do, when the dogs heralded Abram's return.

Filled almost to bursting, Abram bounded into the house, ready to tell me of all the wonders of his trip only to find me rolled in a quilt on the parlor daybed. It took only a short while for him to realize that I simply felt too ill to pay attention.

I explained in my croaking voice where Nancy Hanks was and insisted he go immediately and fetch her. Typical Abram, he did not hesitate but called straightaway for Moses to hitch a wagon.

Mary begged to accompany him, pleading her case that she had been cooped up and overworked as well without Nancy Hanks but I reminded her that her father, after just returning from a long, arduous trip, had a four hour drive ahead of him and would be fortunate to return by nightfall. Vegetables had to be prepared and meat put on to cook and only a single loaf of bread remained since Nancy Hanks had been absent on baking day.

Abram left without delay, carrying two slices of bread wrapped around a thick wedge of cold pork that he would eat on the way. He was home, and Nancy Hanks would soon be back so I allowed myself to doze on my daybed for the remainder of the afternoon, partly from relief, and partly from the soothing qualities of a large dose of my sore throat remedy, although I would never have admitted that to anyone but myself.

The sun had already begun to fade when they arrived. The younger children gathered around Nancy

Hanks, tugging at her skirts, demanding she listen to accounts of what they had done in her absence while Mary, Lizzie and Meggie expressed their relief and joy that she was back.

Amidst it all, I managed to pat her shoulder when she stooped to straighten my covers but I'm sure she could tell by my face how pleased I was to see her.

The welcoming furor had begun to fade when Nancy Hanks turned and stooped to pick up Jane's rag doll from the floor. On the back of her dress, which I knew to be her next to best one, was a dark stain.

"Goodness, Nancy Hanks, how on earth did you soil the back of your dress?"

She twisted around to look and said, "I'm sorry, Mrs. Enloe. Polly and I climbed the hill behind her house this morning and on our way back down, I lost my footing and fell."

"Well," I said. "Thank goodness you didn't turn an ankle. I truly don't know how we'd manage with you and me both unable to get around. Not to say that that is the only reason, you understand."

By the next morning I was on the mend, and by the afternoon I was sipping broth and sorting through my mending basket in anticipation of returning to normal in a few days.

Abram held off on telling me about his trip as long as he could. On his third day home, I was still on the day bed, a blanket draped over my legs but well enough to attempt repairing a badly torn trouser knee, when he sat down beside me and began to talk.

I did not doubt his evaluation of the new land and what it offered for, to his credit, Abram had never been one to overstate even when it could help his cause. I could see that he was captivated by the possibilities but I felt compelled to respond honestly.

"I cannot help but believe the whole idea is based on a foolish desire for adventure and that it is an unnecessary move. We have everything here and acres of land that has never felt the plow or been grazed over. We could live here for a score of years and continue to prosper."

But, being certain that he had already made up his mind, I stated my condition that I had arrived at weeks before after a great deal of deliberation. "A cabin must be built and ready for us when we arrive. I'll sleep in a wagon on the journey because I have to, but not after we get there."

A great wave of relief swept over his face and he reached over and hugged me.

"You won't be sorry, I promise you, Sarah."

"Yes, yes...Abram, who'll be going with us besides the Walkers?"

"Can't say right now," he said. "But Felix and I mean to raise the matter amongst the Puzzle Creek folks in a few days."

Abram began immediately to draw out plans for a new cabin. It would be just like our present home, with the exception of a fifth bedroom that I insisted be added to the ground floor. Abram seemed surprised at my request.

I said, "Well, I, for one, would welcome fewer trips up the stairs. And neither of us is getting any younger."

Abram winced at my words, which surprised me. He had never seemed to be bothered by the idea of aging, but he was a practical realistic man and must needs acknowledge the inevitable sometimes.

Soon a letter arrived from Felix Walker saying that the land had been purchased and the deeds duly filed. This news plunged us into a near-frenzy of plans and preparations that rarely slowed down until our last day.

Abram had completed his drawings for the new cabin and went over and over them with William Gwynn. Gwynn was to take three men, one of them a stone mason, and begin building immediately. They were to use one of our wagons for the necessary building tools and for supplies, including corn and oats for Abram's workhorses. I suppressed a smile as I listened to his repeated instructions on how the team was to be watered, fed and rested regularly.

"I declare," I said as the wagon rolled away. "You're more concerned with the horses than you are the men driving them."

With a wry, half-smile, he said, "The men know how to take care of themselves. The horses know how to follow orders and work. Many a good animal has been ruined by an impatient and careless man."

The departure of William Gwynn seemed to signal an inevitability about our moving that I had not felt before. As I walked through our home I realized that there was no way I intended to leave my furniture behind. There was the linen press, armoire and four-poster rice carved bed that Abram had ordered from Charleston. The parlor furniture had come later but was no less precious to me. In the kitchen, oak chairs made by Josiah Duncan lined one side and each end of a great table made from thick chestnut boards joined so tightly they appeared as one. On the wall side a long bench provided seating for five and allowed the table to be pushed against the wall except at mealtimes. Planing had smoothed the table top in the beginning but nearly twenty years of everyday use had kept it that way. How many meals had we eaten here? How many loaves of bread had been kneaded on its surface? I remembered well how massive it had looked when I first entered the house, but also how quickly it   filled up as years passed. No, I could not leave it behind.

I could concede some of the furniture, especially the children's beds and the schoolroom desks and stools. Simple, sturdy beds were easy enough to build by attaching support boards from the corner of the room down two sides of the walls. A post would be attached to the floor for the outer corner on which would rest the frame. Wooden slats or ropes placed across the frame, then fitted with a corn shuck pad and a feather mattress made a very comfortable sleeping arrangement.   We had never changed over to freestanding beds for the children and I was sure it would not take long to rebuild them in our new home. The schoolroom desks were made of split logs about six inches thick, attached to the wall, flat side up and supported by two legs. The accompanying stools were simply split logs, also flat side up, but with four slanted sapling legs. George and Moses were very adept at this kind of work and I had no doubt that beds and desks and stools could be duplicated in all due haste once we arrived at our new home.

When I informed Abram of my resolution about the furniture, he shook his head but said very little except that we would need two extra wagons. If I had thought it an insurmountable hardship, I would have hesitated to persist. But, I must admit, I took a small, wicked pleasure in getting my way because it seemed to ease some of my remaining inner conflict toward the move.

In the middle of our moving chaos, Felix Walker arrived accompanied by a young man named Samuel Horton, the son of an old friend, who, from what I could gather, was interested in politics and sought to learn what he could from association with Felix. I was tired and left them alone after a bit of polite conversation. I instructed Nancy Hanks to serve them some cider in about an hour. After rising from my rest, I found her in the kitchen, unusually idle and quiet. When I finally managed to draw her out, she admitted that our young visitor had paid unwelcome attention to her with which she was very uncomfortable. After learning that those attentions consisted of standing and bowing and opening the door, I could hardly disguise my amusement.

"She'll never get a husband this way," I thought. "And, she could certainly do worse."

But, as I admitted to Abram later, Horton was a bit of a dandy both in dress and manner. He responded but little, saying that he feared Felix was wasting his time with such a fellow.

We began another round of assessment of our needs for the move. Most of our breakable items and our food needed to be packed in hogsheads, of which we had not nearly enough. Also, there was the question of the extra wagons needed for the furniture. It all came together when Abram decided that he must evaluate the livestock and sell all but the best. By the time all of the families' livestock were combined, even experienced drovers would have difficulty in managing such a large herd, especially on the kind of trails we would be traveling. My only request was that he not sell my two favorite cows which would provide milk on our journey.

The Yadkin was the closest market, although the stock would bring a better price in Charleston or even the Watauga Settlement. So, Abram left with a herd of horses, cattle, and hogs on a drive that would take him at least a week.

With Abram gone, our pace slowed down for we had packed almost everything we could until we had more containers, or more wagons. It suddenly occurred to me that before too long, we would be far, far away from family and friends. So I decided to take Mary, Lizzie, and Meggie and visit my parents one last time before we left. On our way into Puzzle Creek, I thanked God that Abram had not wanted to move to Kentucky, not that it wouldn't have been good to be closer to our Nancy. But Abram had assured me that the distance to Harrodsburg from our new home would be considerably less than from Puzzle Creek, at least after a wagon trail was fully opened. A wagon road had been in existence between Asheville and Kentucky for several years.

We stayed three nights at my parent's home and visited with many of our friends. As we left, there were tears all around, even in my father's eyes. We said goodbye not knowing how long it might be before we saw each other again, if ever.

Abram had found a ready market for the livestock and so had arrived home late the previous day. He had bought two new wagons and had filled them with hogsheads in which we could safely pack much of our small household articles, especially those breakable or easily damaged.

Abram went in to Puzzle Creek and was finally able to give me the names of the families who would be going with us. I was happiest to hear that the Battle's eldest son and his wife were on the list. Others in the family might follow, a pleasant thought, for they had been our close friends for many years.

We began another round of packing, in earnest now that we had containers. I was truly amazed at the possessions we had accumulated over the years, but I could not see even one that could be left behind. All the blue dishes were gone from the Welsh cupboard and I stood running my hand across its empty shelves.

"What a pity we can't take it with us," I said aloud, thinking myself alone.

Abram sighed from the doorway and shook his head.

"Would you be wanting me to dismantle the entire house and haul it along?"

In a voice sharper than I really felt, I said, "Don't tempt me!"

In the middle of all the activity, I remembered my chickens and told Abram that we must take some of them, not only for use along the way but to start a new flock at our new home. He protested mildly but soon came around and sent Moses to build a large hickory slat basket that could be hooked to the side of one of the wagons. The bottom of the basket could be opened to the ground so the chickens could scratch in the soil while we were camped along the way. I tied a piece of red yarn around one leg of six of the best laying hens and the youngest rooster to make sure they did not end up in the pot on our journey.

After the chicken issue was resolved, I started taking cuttings of my apple and plum trees, and digging Horseradish, Rhubarb, and Asparagus roots. I had been careful to save plenty of vegetable, herb and flower seeds, which I packed deep in one of the hogsheads that contained kitchen utensils. The fruit tree cuttings and the roots I wrapped first in wet log moss and then in oiled deerskin to keep them from drying out. At least I could hope to recreate a part of my gardens at our new home place.

We were in the springhouse trying to decide what should be left for the new tenants when I suddenly thought of Joseph and William in Charleston.

"You know," I said. "Maybe we should have brought them home. They would have loved all the commotion of moving."

Abram's response was unusually terse as he responded that it was best that their education not be interrupted.

Finally the morning came when the last of our possessions were loaded on the wagon and there was no more to do except leave. I asked Abram once more if he was sure the Fords would look after everything properly and he assured me again that they would.

The row of heavily loaded wagons filled the road almost to the first bend. As I took one last look, the place seemed already strange to me. The windows of the house were dark, the pastures empty, and the barn appeared abandoned without the plow and wagon that nearly always sat in front. I heard a tiny sob and turned to see Nancy Hanks with tears on her pale cheeks.

"Of course," I thought. She would feel it as much or more than we, for it has been her only real home."

I climbed into my wagon, which George would drive. After tying his five brood mares to the back of the wagons, Abram mounted and rode to the front of the train without looking back.

The wagons began to move in succession and soon the last one had rounded the bend and we were on our way to the Ocona Lufta wilderness.

<u>Nancy Hanks</u>

The Enloe house seemed almost empty with Nancy gone, which was ridiculous because there remained seven children in addition to Mr. and Mrs. Enloe and myself. Nancy had been a very established presence in my life, indeed, the only person I had ever been close to. But I told myself that I must begin to control my feelings and learn not to let them show for I sensed that Mrs. Enloe was tiring of my constant sighs.

Mr. Enloe seemed the most affected for he and Nancy had spent a great deal of time together. He began to speak of news he had heard in Puzzle Creek about how many families were leaving the area for Kentucky and even some for the lands west of the Blue Ridge. Mrs. Enloe listened patiently to his stories but chided him sharply one day when he forgot to pick up a bolt of toweling from the store in Puzzle Creek. She would not discuss the movers, many of whom she had known all her life, but she did not object to hearing him speak at length about them. I could not help feeling some sympathy for him because it was obvious that he was greatly excited by all the talk of new lands.

Life continued in much the usual way, even for the younger children, for they had their assigned chores and their daily lessons that could not be cast aside just because their eldest sister had gone away.

One of my chores was gathering eggs from Mrs. Enloe's sizeable flock of hens. They were never penned up during the day and so laid their eggs wherever they chose. I had made my usual rounds of where I knew nests existed but as I walked by the barn, a hen flapped and cackled her way down from the hayloft. I found the nest of five eggs in the corner of the loft behind a pile of old boards. I carefully made my way back down the steep ladder but as I neared the bottom, my foot slipped, the basket flew out of my hands, and the precious eggs went flying.

Arms from out of nowhere caught me and held me off the ground. I realized instantly that it was Mr. Enloe and I remember wondering why he was whirling me around and around, and then I saw his face. My breath caught in my throat and I could not make a sound, but only look at him in wonder. His arms were strong and warm and I experienced a sensation that I had never felt before. The warmth of his body traveled to my face as he slowly loosened his arms and let my feet slip to the floor. Still I could not speak but simply grabbed the egg basket and fled toward the house.

Mrs. Enloe was in the kitchen and was astonished at my red face and flustered motions. She readily accepted my explanation that I had fallen and broken the eggs. She patted my shoulder and said, "Goodness, Nancy Hanks, don't take on so! We can live with the loss of a few eggs."

As days passed I could almost feel Mr. Enloe looking at me when I was setting the table or kneading bread or going about my other household chores. I was grateful when he suspended school for a couple of weeks so the children could have a break from studying. The thought of sharing the small space of the schoolroom with him was almost painful to me. I tried not to look at him but sometimes I failed. I also failed at convincing myself that the incident in the barn was meaningless. Maybe it was to him, but to me it was the most genuine thing that had ever happened to me. At night I closed my eyes and went through the motions again and again. It had seemed to last so long when it happened but I knew it was only a matter of seconds. As days passed my affection for him grew stronger instead of waning. I tried to avoid him without seeming obvious to Mrs. Enloe but it was not easy.

A few days later Mr. Felix Walker came for a visit and the conversation was all about available land in western North Carolina and the pleasures and challenges of wilderness life. Mrs. Enloe was a bit quieter than usual and participated little in the discussion.

Three days later, Mr. Enloe left very early to join Mr. Walker on a hunting trip. They would be gone for five days so on the second day Mrs. Enloe took the opportunity to take all but Jane and Essie, the youngest two children, to call on the Battles and visit with her family in Puzzle Creek. The next day, I had completed all my other chores, the children were napping, and I was taking loaves of potato bread from the hearth when the door opened and Mr. Enloe walked in. Turning my face from him, I explained Mrs. Enloe's absence as I moved the loaves aimlessly around the table. He moved closer and put his hands on my shoulders. That was all it took to send me into a outburst of passion and I turned and clasped his body with both arms. He smelled of wood smoke and horses and leather and his arms felt as they had in the barn.

I was a collection of conflicting emotion. I was afraid, I was not afraid; I wanted to laugh, I wanted to cry; I was ashamed, I gloried in my wanting of him. My pleasure at least equaled his and in my innocence and lack of experience I was sure that I must be the only person in the world who had ever felt this way. Afterwards we lay silently in each other's arms.

Already the enormity of our actions began to prey on me. A thousand emotions assailed me in the coming days, as my mind was never free from thoughts of him. I came to suppose that our actions were my fault because I had not resisted him. But that was the quandary; I did not want to resist! I could not find anything shameful about our relationship, hard though I tried. Wrong, yes, but strangely, not shameful. I could not help but remember my mother and her situation. I had seen the agreement she signed when she left me with the Enloes. The word 'unmarried' was there and could not be denied. Was I like her? Was there some deep-seated moral flaw in my nature? Should I throw myself in the millpond for my sins? No matter how I tried, I always came back to the starting place.

So, sweet gentle Mr. Enloe was never far from my thoughts. He began to spend so much of his time at hard physical work that Mrs. Enloe remarked that he must surely be struggling with the decision about resettling.

At the end of the week, Mr. Walker and Mr. Enloe left for the west to explore the property they might later purchase. After only one day I was lonely for the sight of him. After almost a week, Mrs. Enloe, correct about my misery but not about the reason for it, suggested that I might take a few days to visit Polly Price in Duncan's Creek. Polly and I had never been especially close but had enjoyed each other's company in a casual way. I was glad to leave the Enloe's for a while because I thought it might help me to gain control of my emotions. It was not to be. I had only been there five days when Mr. Enloe appeared with the news that his wife was ill and desired my immediate return. After we were out of sight of the Price's, I tried to speak, to tell him that I blamed myself for our actions, but instead I began to cry. He drove the wagon off the road into a grove of huge pine trees and turned to console me.

We lay on a spongy carpet of pine needles and shared what we both had come to be possessed by, our passion for each other. Afterwards I was able to speak plainly and clearly for the first time since our initial meeting in the barn. I did not want him to feel pressured by our situation but I wanted him to be certain of my deepest love for him. He looked at me with clear unwavering eyes that openly revealed what he thought and felt and I believed him.

"I'm ashamed," he said, "that I have allowed my emotions to run out of control. But, Nancy, I regard you with a passion so deep it overwhelms me, makes me forget everything, washes over and tosses me like the ocean waves toss a paper boat!"

I answered that my regard for him was so strong that, if needs be, it would last me for the remainder of my life even if we could never be together again.

"I could leave," I said, and immediately realized the foolishness of the offer.

Mr. Enloe would not hear of it. And it was an irrational suggestion. I was still a bondservant and not free to simply pick up and go. Anything other than utter silence and all would be revealed and what a colossal tragedy that would be.

Mrs. Enloe seemed happy to see me as the children flocked around asking questions about my trip.

"Nancy Hanks! How on earth did you soil the back of your good dress?"

The words caught me off guard and my calm voice belied the turmoil churning in my breast.

"Polly and I climbed the hill behind her house this morning and on our way back down I lost my footing and fell."

"Well," said Mrs. Enloe. "Thank goodness you didn't turn an ankle!"

Soon Mr. Enloe brought up the idea of resettling to his wife. She made no attempt to hide her displeasure at the idea but she did not protest very adamantly. However, she plainly stated that she refused to go unless a cabin could be built and ready to move into on their arrival. Perhaps Mr. Enloe had anticipated her demand for he hastily drew up plans that mirrored their present home. Mrs. Enloe insisted on another bedroom on the ground floor, because, she said, "We're not getting any younger!"

I sensed that her statement bothered him some, not the one about the extra room but the reminder of his age.

Soon word came from Mr. Walker that the land had been purchased and deeds filed. The next day William Gwynn, Mr. Enloe's foreman, left with three other men for the Ocona Lufta, but not before Mr. Enloe had gone over several times how they were to make sure the horses that pulled the wagon full of tools were watered, fed and rested properly. At the last minute, he added another bucket of oats to the barrel on the wagon, "Just in case."

Mrs. Enloe chuckled and said, "You treat those horses better than most men treat their wives."

Mr. Enloe smiled dryly but I did not hear his response. However, I knew what she said was true for the only time I had ever seen him really angry was when an itinerant worker was helping to build a new springhouse and tried to drag four times the normal load of rocks with one horse hitched to the stone boat. Nancy and I were not close enough to hear their words but the man left straightaway and Mr. Enloe strode toward the house, his face like a thundercloud.

Much of our normal work was halted because planning, sometimes again and again, demanded a lot of time. I made myself as useful as I could but I suppose my most valuable contribution was keeping the younger children occupied and out of the way.

Mr. Walker returned and brought deeds and maps and a young man who was introduced as Mr. Samuel Horton. Out of curiosity I glanced at him briefly. He was finely dressed, too finely for a visit to a place like the farm. His shirt was Irish linen instead of broadcloth, his breeches and coat of a rich blue velvety material that I had never seen before. Shiny buckles adorned his shoes, and I was soon to see that his affected manners matched his appearance.

Mrs. Enloe stayed in the parlor for only a few minutes but instructed me to serve the men some cider in about an hour while she went up to her bedroom to rest. I did not knock but opened the parlor door quietly and proceeded to the tea table, which Mr. Walker's friend almost tipped over by rising so quickly. He offered a most exaggerated bow that I did not acknowledge and after I had poured the cider, he hurried to the door and held it open for me, again bowing in his pretentious manner. A glance back into the room revealed that Mr. Horton's actions had not escaped Mr. Enloe for he had a most peculiar expression on his face. Later when I mentioned my annoyance at his attentions, Mrs. Enloe seemed amused and said, "You could do worse, Nancy Hanks. But, I do admit, he was a simpering sort of fellow."

Every day seemed to bring some new problem to be dealt with. Mr. Enloe agreed to move the furniture that Mrs. Enloe felt she could not leave behind. To accommodate it, he planned to buy wagons in the

Yadkin where he would take much of his livestock to sell.

The farm was quieter than I ever remembered it with so much of the livestock gone and no Mr. Enloe splitting and chopping and hammering at something all the time. Mrs. Enloe was unusually quiet but soon explained her silence by saying that she had suddenly realized that if she did not see her family now, she might not see them again for a very long time. So she took Mary, Lizzie, and Meggie and left for Puzzle Creek early the next morning. During the days I busied myself with the children's lessons and all the other necessary chores, but at night I lived over and over my experience with Mr. Enloe.

The children and I were engrossed in comparing leaves and flowers that we had gathered to drawings done by a botanist named Michaux who had traveled through the mountains just twenty years before. Joseph and William had sent us tracings from his book to use in our lessons.

We were all startled when Mr. Enloe surprised us with an early arrival from his livestock trip. Our class ended, for the children were much more excited by their father's return than by comparing leaves to drawings. I explained Mrs. Enloe's absence and went to the kitchen to begin our evening meal. Mr. Enloe seemed not to notice my silence during our meal and instead concentrated on his children's numerous and varied questions about the coming trip. I saw the children to bed and went back to tidy the kitchen. I had finished and started upstairs when Mr. Enloe came out of the parlor and motioned for me to come near. He did not touch me but simply leaned forward and whispered in my ear.

Later in the barn, the hay was sharp through my thin dress but it was only a passing irritant. My truthful mind told me I should have to suffer a true scourge, real punishment, but my deceitful one said "Enjoy, take pleasure now, for it will not endure."

Mrs. Enloe and the girls arrived in mid-morning the next day. Mr. Enloe had brought two new wagons and several hogsheads from the Yadkin so she wasted no time in beginning another round of packing in earnest. We used towels and sheets and even clothing to wrap fragile items while more sturdy items were simply stacked together. Mr. Enloe saved us from making a tedious mistake by reminding us of how heavy a hogshead full of iron pots and pans would be to load on to a wagon. So the empty hogsheads were loaded on the respective wagons and we carried our goods by the armloads and handed them up to Mrs. Enloe to place them where they would not be seen again until the end of our journey.

Mr. Enloe went to Puzzle Creek and returned with a list of the families who would be resettling. Mrs. Enloe was happy to see that the Battle's oldest son was on the list. As for myself, the person I most wanted to accompany us was already living happily in Kentucky.

Finally the day came when only a few pots, plates, and dishes and our sleeping covers that we would need on our journey were left unpacked. Mr. Enloe announced that we would leave early the following day.

After breakfast the next morning I went outside and watched the sun come up over the farm. I found it difficult to believe that I might never see it again. I wandered around almost in a state of confusion until Mrs. Enloe called me to help round up the little ones, James, Jane and Essie, and get them into her wagon that George would drive. Samuel, Daniel, and I would ride with Moses and since they were older, Mary, Lizzie, David, and Meggie would ride in whichever wagon had room for them.

Mrs. Enloe commented that my face was pale and asked if I was well.

"Yes," I assured her. "Just tired and excited."

"Well," she said, "Maybe we can all get some rest on the trip. At least it will be a change from this infernal packing."

I had promised myself that I would not look back once we began to move but I felt compelled to turn my eyes toward the place that had provided my greatest happiness and my greatest torment. The farm was still, not an animal or person moved and no breeze rustled the trees. It was like staring at a lifeless painting. Samuel and James soon drowned out the crunch of the wagon wheels with their excited speculations about what adventures we might encounter on the trip. I bit my lip and stared straight ahead. We were on our way.

Chapter Three

From Puzzle Creek to Asheville

Early August 1803 found the Enloes on the outskirts of Puzzle Creek joining the other families and their wagons. Each was drawn by a pair of oxen except for two of the Enloe's heaviest wagons that were a yoke of four. Most families had culled their cattle and hogs, keeping only the best stock. Each animal bore its owner's mark or brand and so all could be driven in a common herd. There were plenty of young men and boys to help with the livestock but experienced drovers were in charge. They were the ones who knew how to keep the animals in a collective herd at night, safe from lions they called 'cattymounts' and wolves that seemed to lurk just out of sight any time the wagons halted.

The drovers rode horses that did not shy at the approach of a steer or even a massive grunting boar. Indeed, some of them could chase down, rope, and hold a large cow with the help of their horses which they called 'quarters' because of their ability to sprint for a short distance at a high speed.

Abram Enloe and a few of the other men rode horses suitable for traveling instead of working stock. Other men walked beside their oxen and occasionally changed places with a family member on the wagon seat. What brought them together as one was the reason for the exodus. Their purpose was the same, although many of them would find it difficult to verbalize. Excitement and anticipation lay ahead in a new land where they would be the first white settlers, for only trappers and hunters had penetrated that far. Good land waited where they could create a more prosperous life for their families and their descendants. Many looked forward to the sense of freedom that comes with being far away from the mundane problems of life in a settlement or village. With no exception they were aware of the dangers facing them for almost all of them had braved the wilderness before. Far away from settlements meant no doctor, no church, no store, constant war with wild animals and the elements, and until the first crops came in, living on wild game supplemented by the few staples they had been able to bring with them. Their exhilaration at certain adventure topped the possibilities of danger and hardship and their voices rang with excitement as they began their journey.

The first day after leaving Puzzle Creek, the train covered only twenty miles. They had not left until the sun was high. After the first day, they fell into a pattern of sorts and, except for the landscape, one day was much the same as the next. Everyone had been informed that no stops would be made to cook a midday meal and that some kind of dried meat or other prepared food would be necessary. In the evening they stopped the wagons while enough light remained for young boys to gather wood for a communal fire. Then each family built a small cooking fire near its supply wagon. Most pots contained stew made from dried beef, or cured pork with root vegetables such as potatoes, carrots, parsnips, turnips, and onions. Some women baked flat bread on iron skillets, others potato bread in Dutch ovens settled into the hot coals. The rich smell of coffee was an invitation to the drovers who rotated, eating with a different family each night. Some families had brought soft cider for their children, others depended upon spring water which was to be located within a matter of a few feet almost anywhere along the trail. Still others milked cows each morning and night and shared the excess with whoever needed it.

Nathan Plott owned a unique breed of hounds that were great trackers. Every few days he would leave the trail with his dogs and return with a deer that would be skinned and dressed, stewed in a large kettle, and shared by all the company.

At night the communal fire was banked with large dry hardwood logs that were plentiful in the surrounding forest, usually the results of lightning strikes. Pine started easily and heated quickly but also burned up rapidly. Hardwood burned slowly through the night leaving plentiful coals for starting cooking fires each morning.

The nights were balmy and most men and boys slept on the ground. Women and girls slept inside the wagons on mattresses of corn shucks or feathers that would be transferred to beds in their new homes. The men took turns standing watch each night.

After several days of rolling hills and long valleys, the trail to Asheville became a seemingly unending series of immense gorges walled by steep mountains so high their summits were hidden from view. Once, the men halted the wagons and they all gaped in wonder at a great stone monolith that resembled a giant chimney. One evening some of the most adventurous boys wandered off to explore and returned with an exciting tale of a huge cave that spouted thousands of bats from its mouth.

Sometimes what seemed an insurmountable range of mountains rose before them but as they moved ahead the trail would ease into a gap that allowed their passage. Delays were common but none were lengthy. With the cooperation of men and horses and oxen, any obstacle could be removed from the trail, be it a great tree or a gigantic boulder.

One evening when the train moved through a saddle and topped out on a treeless ridge, an eerie sight lay in the valley before them. Long ago a fire had ravaged the area. The new vegetation was lush and green and of great variety. But all over the valley large dead trees, bleached snow white by decades in the sun, glowed in the evening light as their skeletal fingers reached up through the undergrowth toward the sky.

Abram Enloe looked on the sight and, although the day was warm, a shiver swept over his body. Was it an omen, he thought, a forecast of things to come? He shook off the feeling and turned his thoughts to more controllable matters.

Soon the train reached an area where, unlike the ups and downs they had encountered on the first leg of the journey, they began a long steady climb that was much steeper than it appeared. The trail was open with few problem areas but their progress was slowed sometimes to a crawl. Finally, after what seemed an interminable passage of time, the landscape leveled out somewhat and by the end of the next day, ahead of them in a wide bowl-shaped valley appeared the settlement of Asheville. First named Morristown, its name had been changed to honor Samuel Ashe, governor of North Carolina from 1795 to 1798. The same French Broad River that Abram Enloe and Felix Walker had crossed during their exploratory journey ran very near the town although it had become much wider and deeper as it snaked its way north.

The men drew their wagons together outside the town and the drovers gathered the cattle and hogs into a large corral made of thick heavy brush and tree branches that had obviously been used by previous travelers. Tired from the steep climb, the oxen and cattle settled immediately but the hogs grunted impatiently for their daily ration of corn and the chickens clucked to be put down on fresh dirt.

Exhausted from the day's journey, no one ventured into the town that night. The next morning the men examined their wagons and harness to find any wear or damage so it might be repaired for the second leg of the journey. Children ran and played noisily, happy in the knowledge that they would not be moving on again that day. The women took stock of their cooking supplies, salt and other seasonings, knowing that this was the only place on the journey where they might be replenished.

After the midday meal, Sarah Enloe and Nancy Hanks joined their neighbors in a visit to Morrison's Store, a large one-level building with a flat roof, high in front and low in the back. Inside, in lieu of interior walls, large support columns made of massive peeled poplar logs stood here and there, their sides worn shiny by men who leaned against them while their womenfolk looked and bought.

Across the back were stacks of deer, bear and other animal hides. Shelves and large wooden pegs were laden with axes, saws, hatchets, chisels, hoes spades, wedges, nails, door locks, fierce animal traps, grindstones, whetstones, knives, horseshoes, saddlery, harness, tobacco, strop razors and fishhooks.

Another row of shelves held paper and ink, needles, ribbon, lace, thread, shoe buckles, buttons, flat irons, iron candlesticks, skillets, pots, dutch ovens, fire tongs, and scissors.

Sarah had never seen the like of yard goods, not even on her trips to the markets with Abram. Long tables held bolt after bolt of baize, cambrick, Durant, fustian, wool worsted, shallom, oznabrig, linen, lawn and even silk.

Another area held spices, spirits, sugar, salt, and other non-perishable foodstuffs. Still another was filled with shoes, stockings, hats, earrings and necklaces and even used books. A small area was sectioned off and served as a post office.

Asheville lay in an area where settlers came from many directions and had need of supplies before continuing to the Watauga Settlement, through the Cumberland Gap into Kentucky and the Ohio country, and, of late, even west to Missouri and beyond. There were other settlements with trading posts but no one place that could fill a settler's every need like Morrison's.

While Abram spoke with the storeowner and several other men about what they knew of the trail from Asheville to their destination, Sarah and Nancy Hanks gathered their small purchases and returned to the wagons. Although some rest was to be had during the one-day stop, the train would leave the next morning so an early evening would be beneficial for all. One of the drovers winked and tipped his hat at an oblivious Nancy Hanks as she and Sarah passed by the corral. Sarah smiled to herself.

"The child will never get a husband that way."

Before the sun rose the next morning, the air was filled with a not too unpleasant cacophony made in the effort to start the wagon train moving. Cooking pots banged as they were strapped on wagon sides, and drovers yelled instructions to each other and the livestock. Oxen lowed as yokes were laid across their shoulders, hogs grunted, rooting for one last morsel and chickens squawked at being closed up in their baskets. Doused breakfast fires sizzled and a last minute hammer on a loose horseshoe rang out like a starting bell.

Suddenly a new sound rose above it all as a young man on horseback rode toward them waving a piece of paper over his head.

"Enloe? Who is Enloe?"

Abraham Enloe already being at the front of the train, his wife stepped forward.

"I'm Mrs. Abram Enloe."

"Well, it's for you, Ma-am. Come in last night but you'd all turned in so Mr. Morrison said deliver it this morning."

Accepting the letter, Sarah thanked the young man as Nancy Hanks and the other children crowded around.

"Yes," she said. "Yes, it's from our Nancy. But, we'll wait until your father can join us to open it."

The train moved out before the sun was up. The trail west from Asheville was narrow and skirted the Broad River's edge for several miles until it reached a wide shallow crossing. The wagons groaned as their wheels sank into the sand but the gravel bottom held firm and as the oxen pulled their loads out of the water the settlers turned their backs to the rising sun and headed southwest.

Harrodsburg, Kentucky
8 July 1803

My Dear Parents,

By the time this reaches you, you may already be in your new home. I have directed that Mr. Battle forward this letter to the Asheville Post if you have already begun your journey, and that the Asheville Post hold it until called for by one of the family or an emissary.

What an exciting time it must have been making ready for such an undertaking! I can imagine all the planning and packing and work. Mother, did you win Father over on the matter of your furniture? Father, please let me know which horses you kept and I will gladly give you my opinion of your choices. And what of George and his precious beehives? I cannot believe he would agree to leave them behind. In fact, with great merriment I imagine him sitting stubbornly by his hives as you all go out of sight down the road.

Alas, I have brought to mind a scene that I must admit saddens me. The thought that I might never see my dear home again had never occurred to me until I received your letter. It being the only home that I and all my brothers and sisters have ever known, and now filled with strangers, brings tears to my eyes. But, I must steel myself against such unproductive emotion and accept that life is an ever-changing chain of events.

How is dear Nancy Hanks taking the move? Please tell her I will write directly to her when time allows. We have also been busy finishing our cabin and taking care of all those many unanticipated chores that must be done here because of the continued (though very slight) threat of Indian attacks. The men make sport of us women when we worry but I notice they pay particular attention to those precautions that will help to keep us all safe.

Something of a surprising nature to me is the numbers of people who have come here from the Carolinas, both years ago and of late. There are many familiar names from the Yadkin and Watauga Settlements, Bryan, Munday, Lincoln, Carter, Hays, Horton, Berry, Ingram, Isaacs, Hanks and Marshal, to name only a few. However, you may have heard that the most famous resident, a hero of yours, Father, moved west to Missouri almost four years ago. I speak, of course, of Colonel Daniel Boone, as he is so referred to here. Even in his absence he is still well loved and held in great esteem by those who knew him. His only detractors are the relatives of a man called Richard Callaway who apparently was always jealous of Colonel Boone and caused him much grief over many petty differences.

Now I will fulfill my promise to describe the Kentucky countryside. It is beautiful and endowed with a rich limestone soil that grows lush grass finer than anywhere in the country, so say the settlers from eastern Virginia, of which there are many. Your horses, Father, would grow fat and lazy on such pasture. The thick meadows look blue from a distance and the area is already being called 'The Bluegrass.'

There are streams and creeks everywhere, Father, which would satisfy your love for building gristmills and forges. Perhaps Kentucky would have suited your purposes better than the Ocona Lufta. But, I know well your love of the wilderness, and indeed, Colonel Boone is said to have left here because the true wilderness is no more to be found in this area.

My dear parents, duty calls and Arthur awaits this letter, as he is ready to travel to Harrodsburg where he will see it posted. Please kiss my brothers and sisters and dear Nancy Hanks for me. When you have time to answer, please send the address of my brothers in Charleston that I may correspond with them.

Your loving daughter,
Nancy Enloe Thompson

Chapter Four

From Asheville to Ocona Lufta

The trail from Rutherford County to Asheville had been scenic, interesting and sometimes challenging. From Asheville on it was an adversary that tested the settlers in every way: their skills, courage, patience, physical stamina, ingenuity, or their lack of any of these.

For days the trail would be scarcely wide enough for their large wagons, then would suddenly be reduced to a path that must have barely allowed William Gwynn and his narrow wagon to pass through. The train would halt, all axes would come out and soon the mountains would reverberate like a concert hall with no way to distinguish between what was real and what was echo. Sometimes an entire day was lost, sometimes only a few hours. But they moved on at whatever pace the wilderness allowed and were thankful for the progress made each day.

One day they topped out on a wide ridge and saw before them a high, pointed mountain, its steep sides dotted with only occasional vegetation. For hours the wagon train followed the trail that coiled like a snake around the shoulders of the mountain, plunged down a steep ravine, zigzagged briefly over a rocky saddle, then brought them at almost dusk to a safe place to camp for the night.

Now there was little talk or playfulness around the communal fire. Exhausted and sore, the men ate silently and crawled into their bedrolls early hoping for strength that would carry them through the coming day.

Sometimes they camped on hilltops and were lit by moon and stars. Other times they camped in hollows and gorges with mountainsides so steep their fires barely made a dull glow in the impending darkness. Overhead a few stars shown faintly in the narrow ribbon of sky the ridges permitted them to see. Each day dawned with the uncertainty of what lay ahead. There began grumbling among some of the men that nothing at the end of the journey could be worth the trials of getting there. Abram Enloe let Felix Walker be the one to answer these complaints since he was the politician and more practiced at diplomacy.

The Enloe's foreman, William Gwynn, had traveled the route with his narrow horse drawn wagon and had marked the trail very well by blazing trees so they would be visible quite a way ahead. Once the trail simply ended in a huge gully, obviously created by recent rains. The stream had receded to its normal level but the deep ravines on each side were impassable. Their choices were to retrace several miles and search for a new place to cross or to find some way to rebuild the crossing.

Stacey Wallace, who was the most vocal of the complainers, asked in his shrill voice, "Have you ever considered that this might not be the trail, that we might just be lost? It's been a long time since we saw any sign."

With set jaw guarding against hot words that come easy under stress, Abram Enloe said, "Of course this is the trail."

Wallace spoke again, "Well, I don't see no marks around here."

Enloe walked off from the others and stood alone pondering. He worked his way downstream and after a short search, in a cluster of trees that had been jerked from the ground by the flood waters, found a clump of birches with several large chunks of bark that had obviously been chipped away with an axe. With this discovery, most of the men were in favor of rebuilding instead of searching for a new crossing. They began by rolling large stones into the gullies in a wide straight row that reached across the small stream, all the way to the other side. Then, everyone who was not needed to watch over the livestock pitched in and carried smaller stones to fill in around the large ones. Still smaller stones filled in until a track began to emerge that was wide enough for the wagons. Every container available, from stew pots to Dutch ovens to nail kegs, was used to carry sand from the banks upstream to fill in between the stones on the track. The creek waters ran through the large stones on the bottom and the track remained solid.

Although a few men, Wallace included, voiced their opinion that the track would not hold, Enloe and Walker declared it was best to go ahead and cross before nightfall. After all, one heavy rain upstream during the night and all the work they had done would be for nothing. The track stayed firm under the wagons and they camped that night on a small plateau on the other side.

Although the trail remained wide enough for the wagons for the next several days, the wildness of the area became more apparent and more pronounced. Panthers screamed and wolves howled, piercing the night's stillness and making sleep almost impossible. Sometimes the livestock grew restless and hard to manage and when morning came the drovers and young boys would find wild animal sign around the edges of the camp.

The sounds reminded Sarah of her first nights in the wilderness in Rutherford, the difference being that they had been safe inside their cabin and not sleeping in wagons or on the ground.

Finally the train reached an area that Abram Enloe and Felix Walker could identify on one of their maps. They were nearing a place that the Cherokee Indians called Soco. Enloe rode on ahead and his heart sank as he saw how steeply the earth dropped away and how far the precipitous incline lasted before ending in a gentle slope. Far ahead he could see a large pine that had been blazed, which meant that William Gwynn had come this way. But Gwynn's small wagon pulled by a team of horses was only a quarter of the weight of most of these wagons. The brakes on Gwynn's wagon were strong and had obviously allowed him to ease down the steep mountainside without shoving into the horses. Also, horses were more coolheaded in these situations where oxen were apt to panic, drawing on their ancient propensity for stampeding.

After much the same discussion as at the creek crossing, the men decided that what was needed was something that would act as an extra brake and help to hold back the heavy wagons.

Strong ropes were plentiful but the idea that every man there, acting together, could hold back even the lightest wagon was soon laid to rest. Then someone came up with the idea that if a heavy object could be tied to the back and dragged behind the wagon that might slow it down enough to descend the mountainside safely. The object must by necessity be jagged and rough, for a smooth object would simply slide into the very wagon it was supposed to be holding back.

Abram Enloe walked around in a large grove of hemlock pines and immediately saw that they could be made to work, but he offered his idea quietly as just a possibility. He did not want a repeat of the dissention that had occurred at the creek crossing. After very little discussion, axes appeared and chopping began, chips flying in all directions for, if the idea worked, each wagon would need its own tree brake. The first down was a large hemlock with many branches. When the men began to pull the trunk around to the wagon, Enloe intervened and suggested the top go first so the drag would be stronger as the limbs caught in the soil. Wallace objected only slightly this time, but stood akimbo off to the side, leaning against a tree as though he had little faith in the course of action.

The first wagon started down the incline and with the initial movement the tree slid forward and touched the back of the wagon. Then the tree stopped and stayed there until the oxen began to pull. Soon the wagon was halfway down, leaving behind a trail of deep grooves where the ends of the branches had gouged into the earth.

The wagon came to an easy stop on the gentle slope below and was followed by a great roar of cheers and yells and whistles. Several men jumped on their horses and rushed down to help remove the tree brake and then back up the hill to repeat the process for each of the remaining wagons. Wallace stood back for a while longer and then joined the others but had very little to say.

Late the next day the train reached an area where two large streams plunged separately over a series of rocky ledges for about a hundred feet and formed an almost round catch basin below. They made camp with little time for exploration before nightfall.

The next morning dawned brightly as the sun pierced the leafy green ceiling and cast a glow through the mist surrounding the roaring falls. There were few among the train that did not explore to some extent the surrounding area. It was an Eden with mountain laurel and rhododendron shining like glass through the woods.

All manner of ferns and galax and mosses carpeted the rocks up and down each side of the falls. Gigantic hemlocks grew on top of some of the rocks, their roots on one side sinking deeply into the black loam for stability and sustenance, the other into the edges of the falls for constant moisture. The stream, lined on both sides with columns of silver barked poplars, gurgled its way out of sight into a wooded valley.

Abram Enloe looked on the place with wonder and envy, wishing it were a part of the tract he had bought. However, he needed usable land. To look on beauty was a fine thing, but land had to offer subsistence to render it practical and he knew the land waiting for him would do that and more.

The train camped for two days at the falls giving the bravest of the young men and boys an opportunity to show off their stamina by plunging into the cold water of the basin at the foot of the falls. While the young girls watched the young men dunking each other and competing to see who could remain underwater the longest, many of the older women went to see a great patch of lady slipper, a beautiful and unusual plant the Indians called 'moccasin flower' because the bloom greatly resembled a yellow shoe or slipper.

Needed repairs were made on wagon wheels and harness. Much to Abram Enloe's disappointment, Felix Walker decided he would leave the train and start north for his property on Jonathon Creek instead of going farther west. A trapper named Jonathon McPeters had named the place many years before.

The Kennedys, Harmons and Hollifields would go on with Walker to settle the land surrounding his. The Battles, Plotts, Stoakleys and Wallaces would remain with the Enloes and would file on available land in the area surrounding the Ocona Lufta.

Walker's party moved out at midmorning after warm and sometimes tearful farewells between the young people and some of the women. Nancy Hanks was sorry that the Hollifields were to go with the Walkers but she was pleased that the Battles would be going to the Ocona Lufta for they had been friends of the Enloes for many years.

As the now much smaller train moved onward, impatience began to grow in each breast. Nerves grew taut and confrontations between some of the men were barely averted. They were exhausted and tense with anticipation at this late date; had they made the right decision and even if they hadn't, what could they do about it now? Enloe played the mediator and kept the worst from happening day after day but always felt as if the group was walking on the edge of a precipice.

Then one day in midmorning they reached a small clearing where Enloe and Walker had, what now seemed ages ago, blazed trees to show what directions the other settlers would take to find their parcels of land. All at once calmness settled in and disagreements were cast aside as each family made ready to start out on its own. Livestock had to be sorted out and Enloe gave each family a map showing where its claim laid. There was much congratulating, hand shaking and backslapping as a new eagerness took hold.

The other families decided to move on at once, anxious to be on the way to their place where they would arrive in two days if they started now. Again goodbyes were said among the women and children. Sarah Enloe hugged Mary Battle close and then said, "We won't be too far apart, Mary. After we're settled we'll wear a trail between our places that will be easy to trod."

After the last wagon disappeared, Sarah turned to Abram. "How much further?"

"One more night," he said. "We'll be there by tomorrow afternoon if all goes well."

Abram Enloe stood and looked around at his family, his wagons, cattle, horses, hogs and even the chickens and George's beehives. They had made it and he could now admit to himself that there were times when he had doubted that they would. Of all the original livestock only two shoats, one cow and five of Sarah's chickens had been lost, the hogs and cow to wild animals and the chickens to the stew pot. A few tools had been lost along the way, a few fistfights had arisen over one thing and another. Still, no human lives had been lost and no serious injuries had been incurred. All in all a remarkable record for the extraordinary journey they had made.

As Abram had promised, early the next afternoon as they came out of the woods into a clearing, the cabin appeared before them. The older girls began squealing and jumped from their wagons and began to run across an open meadow that led up to the house. The road had been well worn by repeated trips with wagon and stone boat so the Enloes drove up to the front of their new home and stopped.

Chapter Five

Abram Enloe

The good work William Gwynn and his helpers had done on the new cabin made our arrival and settling in much more simple and pleasant than it might otherwise have been. He had followed my plan and directions to the letter. All logs had been squared off and fitted together so neatly that a minimal amount of daubing had been necessary. Not even the smallest strip of bark remained to encourage insects or decay. The plank floors were a testament to whoever had used an adze to level them. In the spring, glass windows would replace some of the tightly fitting shutters. The chimneys did not smoke and William, on his own initiative, had built sturdy shelves on the kitchen wall where the Welsh cupboard had been in our old home. The cabin seemed very large, at least in its empty state, which meant that Sarah would be able to fit in all her precious furniture with room to spare.

On the afternoon of our arrival, we decided to unload only what was required to cook our evening meal. Pallets on the floor would provide our beds for the night. After breakfast the next morning, we began to unpack in earnest with Sarah deciding where each item would be placed in the house. I left Moses and George to help her and headed out to the wagons that held tools and forge implements, and another that held two large grindstones with which I would soon build a gristmill on the nearby creek.

Nancy Hanks was helping the younger children to gather armloads of their belongings and books and slates for the schoolroom from one of the wagons. I stopped for a moment and helped Samuel lift a wooden crate to the ground. Nancy Hanks looked unusually tired and pale, the result of the long trip, I thought. Although I stood beside her for a moment, she did not speak or look directly at me. It bothered me a bit but I did not force the issue. After all, I was no closer to resolving our problem than I had been before we left Rutherford County.

It took us less than a week to attain some semblance of normalcy from our move. The cabin was so similar to the one we had just vacated that most things went right into place. With her usual approach, Sarah knew exactly where she wanted everything from furniture to pots and pans and that's where they went.

Not all of us were that certain of the space to be occupied. Moses and George argued over where their cabin should be built. George wanted it near the edge of the wood where he had spotted a great stand of sourwood trees that would supply nectar for his precious bees. Moses chose the edge of a meadow that offered a rich garden spot nearby. I left them to it, knowing they would eventually sort it out as they had always done.

Most of the next few weeks I spent choosing sites and making plans for other buildings we would need before winter. A barn was essential and would be built after George and Moses' cabin was completed. Then a springhouse, corn crib, and cellar. Sarah's garden plot could wait for a while for it was too late in the season for seeding most vegetables, although I knew she would want to get her roots and fruit stock into the ground as soon as possible.

We had been on our new property just short of five weeks when the bottom fell out of our world. Nancy Hanks approached me one day when I was out of sight of the house setting posts for a new corral. Her face told me immediately that something was terribly wrong.

In a voice dull as death she told me that she was with child. Then she seemed about to collapse and I held her up, held her against me.

How was it that I could be so starkly silent in the face of such a disaster? I was cold, numb, and lifeless. I could not console Nancy with a solution for I had none. Just questions, endless questions. Why had I, a man with ten children never consciously considered the possibility, no, the likelihood, that this young woman might conceive? Why had I never been realistic about where this situation would likely end? There in the cold light of the present, I admitted to myself that the answer to all these questions was that I had not wanted to consider them. Instead, I had pushed them to the back of my mind to be dealt with in the future. Well, the future was here and again I had no answer, especially to the question of how in God's name I was going to tell Sarah, my wife, about this?

I asked Nancy to try to keep silent for a while and told her that I would find a solution somehow.

Her voice said, "Yes, I will."

Her dismal expression said, "There is no hope."

For days I agonized over how to break such terrible news to Sarah. Words that seemed right one minute seemed trite and cruel the next. She was as dear to me as she had ever been, but how could I expect her to believe that? Days passed and I felt as if I would burst when I was near Sarah, in the parlor, at the table, in our bed, but every time I felt the admission rise within me, I turned away.

The matter lay heavy on my mind and I found myself preoccupied when I tried to turn my hand at any endeavor. Then one day, as I half-heartedly attempted to inspect some harness, I met Sarah as I came out of the barn.

I read her face and before she spoke three words I felt my body grow cold and heavy. After she finished telling me what she had discovered, I realized that she did not yet know the whole truth and, may God forgive me, I entertained the thought that maybe she need not know my involvement. To my credit, that scheme I squelched immediately.

Sarah's question brought me out of my thoughts.

"What's wrong, Abram? Did you already know about this?"

"Sarah," I said. "This is the most difficult thing I've ever had to do. I ask for your forgiveness and your understanding."

Her face changed from anger to concern and then fear as she stood waiting for me to speak.

"Nancy Hanks...the child is mine, Sarah. I'm the father of her child."

I forced myself to face her although decency demanded I turn away in shame. She became unsteady for a moment and fearing that she might fall, I reached out to her. In a fury, she struck at my hand and in the same motion staggered to the corner of the barn. I could hear her retching, while I stood helpless, self-disgraced, and self-dishonored. She looked at me once more in revulsion and disbelief and then ran toward the house.

When I had myself under control, I went inside. Nancy Hanks spoke only a few words to assure me that she had not broken her promise and that Sarah had found out on her own. Then she went about getting Essie and Jane ready for bed in a manner so subdued and silent that even they noticed.

I told the other children that their mother was ill with a severe headache, probably due to the stress of moving, and would remain in the quiet of her room until morning. I kept watch on our bedroom door but it never opened. Indeed, there was no sound at all from within. After the children had all gone to bed, I sank down against the wall beside our door and stayed there the remainder of the night.

Sunlight streaming through the schoolroom window had just awakened me when the bedroom door opened and Sarah appeared. Her face was haggard and pale, her voice quiet and unemotional but resolute.

"We have to talk, Abram. I must hear it all."

We went to the parlor and closed the door. I began to speak, to pour out my transgressions to her and they spilled out like water over a dam. To her credit, she did not interrupt me in any way but sat expressionless until I had offered up every detail. Minutes passed and still she did not speak.

The silence was oppressive and finally I said, "So, where do we go from here?"

My words seemed to break through her emotionless posture and she sprang at me sobbing and hammering at my chest with both fists. I tried to calm her, to comfort her, to say how wretched I was to have been the cause of such grief. She pulled away and fell back into a chair, burying her face in both hands. Silently I waited. I was about to try again but was startled when Sarah spoke in a quiet voice as cold as ice.

"She can't stay here. She must leave now!"

"But, where," I said, "where can she go? She has no family, no one!"

"I don't care where, so long as she is out of my sight. She can live in the woods with the wild animals, for in my estimation, she has acted as such!"

Shocked at vehemence I had never known in her before, I said, "Sarah, would you have me cast her out alone into the wilderness like Hagar?"

She came back at me savagely. "Would you have me live in a house with your concubine as my equal? To be reminded every time I looked at her of your foul infidelity? I cannot! I will not! You must find a way to remove her from here and quickly. The sooner she is out of my sight, the sooner I may regain some peace!"

I quitted the parlor and headed for the woods where I could think without interruption. Finally, Felix came to mind. He would help, but it would take days for him to journey here and I feared the possibilities of what might happen if I did not heed Sarah's order that Nancy Hanks leave immediately. When I had finally worked out the details, I went directly to Nancy, explained, and instructed her to pack her things and make ready to leave within the hour. A sad and miserable wretch I felt at what I was forced to do but God does not always wait to start punishing us for our transgressions. No pain I could go through would ever wipe away the sad, hopeless expression on Nancy's face as she began to gather her belongings.

I tore myself away from her and went to write a letter to Felix. Shame burned my face at every stroke of the pen but I explained the situation truthfully and in detail. I implored him to give Nancy Hanks shelter until further arrangements could be made.

William Gwynn had proven himself to be honest and loyal many times over, so I directed him to hitch up our smallest wagon and make ready to leave for Jonathon Creek as soon as possible.

"This letter is to be delivered directly into Mr. Walker's hands and no one else's," I said. "Wait for an answer no matter how long it takes. William, you will see that no harm comes to Nancy Hanks on the trip?"

I waited outside until Nancy was ready. She had not spoken a word when I told her that she would be going to the Walkers and she remained silent as I helped her into the wagon. In spite of my struggle, I felt a part of myself leaving with her and I knew of a certainty that I would never be whole again. Just before the wagon went out of sight, she turned and looked back for a moment, and then she was gone.

Suffice it to say that the atmosphere around our house was chaotic. Sarah could not speak to me without losing herself to fury or tears. The first civil conversation we had was to discuss what Mary and Lizzie should be told about the reason for Nancy Hanks leaving. We decided that they were old enough to know the truth, although Sarah would not hear of telling them of my part in the debacle. Mary and Lizzie took the news with quiet astonishment. We told the younger children that Nancy Hanks had gone to work for the Walkers. They grumbled and asked who would take Nancy Hanks' place in the classroom? Sarah tried but did not succeed in keeping the terseness from her voice when she answered that we had decided that we no longer needed help.

The next day William Gwynn returned with a letter from Felix Walker. Yes, they would give Nancy Hanks a place for as long as needed. He had told his wife, Phoebe that Nancy was with child but not by whom. He would tell her only if and when it became necessary. My relief was great for at least I would not need to worry for Nancy's safety. I did not let myself look too far into the future for the present was difficult enough to manage.

Sarah became calmer, not her old self by any means, but at least easier with the children. I could see her fighting to retain control when Jane or Essie asked for Nancy. Toward me she remained cold, emotionless, detached. For appearances sake, we slept in the same room, the same bed, but there was a great chasm between us. I did not try to change her feelings toward me for I knew better than anyone what I had done to her and that nothing I could say or do would repair the damage anytime soon, if ever.

I thanked God for the work that lay before me and each day I plunged myself into it with a fury. At night I never closed my eyes in sleep without wondering how Nancy Hanks had fared that day.

An uneasy calm had just settled over our household and Sarah and I found that we could discuss necessary issues with a degree of civility when disaster struck again.

Lena Wallace stopped at our place on her way home from Jonathon Creek where she had been staying with a friend who had gone through a difficult confinement. She had visited the Walkers and seen Nancy Hanks whose condition was now obvious. She took great pleasure in giving Sarah all the details and how the neighbors were all guessing at the name of the father.

Lena Wallace was barely out of sight before Sarah asked me to walk outside with her. We were just out of earshot of the house when she exploded into a trembling rage.

"I can't live with it, Abram. This is the way it's going to be from now on. People like that...that Wallace woman gossiping, smirking, suggesting. Jonathon Creek is only a day's ride away. Every time anyone sees your paramour there I'll have to hear about it. She has to go away, Abram. I don't know or care where, but far away!"

As much as I sympathized with Sarah, I felt just as strongly for Nancy Hanks. Each woman was paying equally for my weakness. With a heavy heart, I wrote again to Felix, asking if he could take Nancy Hanks back to Puzzle Creek. I suggested he first try the Tanners who lived there for it had always been rumored that Nancy's father was a Tanner. If they would not accept her, he was to take her to my tenants, the Fords, along with a letter from me asking them to give her a place in their home at my expense.

Felix wrote back to say that he and his wife had already planned a trip to the Yadkin and would go through Puzzle Creek and see Nancy settled.

Three weeks later, word came from Felix that the Tanners refused their home to Nancy Hanks but that the Fords had accepted her after reading my letter. Sarah seemed relieved at the news but our uneasy peace had suffered a setback.

She said, "So much trouble for so many people because of a ..."

I interrupted before she could say more and reminded her that she was free to heap any criticism and scorn upon me but I would not hear Nancy Hanks maligned for a situation that was not of her own making. Sarah hushed but I sensed that her bitterness for Nancy Hanks had still not reached its full intensity.

Again, life seemed to settle to some extent. The younger children had adjusted to Nancy Hanks' absence, but Mary, Lizzie and Meggie frequently complained about the extra work required of them. Not a day went by that I was not preoccupied with finding a solution for the situation. I wondered constantly if she was well. And my heart ached to think of her alone and with strangers when she had so much to endure.

Winter came, a mild one with little snow and temperatures more like spring. Thankfully, I was able to spend a lot of my time out of doors, away from Sarah's reproachful eyes. Most of our outbuildings were finished and tools readied for spring plowing and planting. Several cows had already calved and my best mare would soon foal. It was toward the end of February when Felix Walker showed up unexpectedly one day. He asked me to show him around the property so we rode to the top of a mountain where we could look down at the house. I could tell that Felix was not there just to admire my farm and I told him so in an unusually brusque manner. He was as ever direct and informed me that a rumor making the rounds in the community accused me of "doing away" with Nancy Hanks.

My astonishment and shock were equaled only by the intense anger that followed. Who could have started such a malignant slander? And why?

Felix's best guess was the Wallaces. Stacey Wallace had resented me ever since I ruled for the other side in a civil suit that he had brought against one of his neighbors in Puzzle Creek. I knew that was why he had taken every opportunity to oppose me on our journey from Rutherford but I would never have imagined that he would start such a heinous rumor over trivial differences.

"Nancy Hanks will have to be brought back here," Felix said. "You'll have to put the lie to this rumor, and be quick about it, whatever the price."

Whatever the price? I knew what that price would be and I knew who would present the bill. At first Sarah was speechless. Then she sank down into a chair and began to sob.

"Will we never be free from this revolting state of affairs? Is there no other way but that she must be brought back here to my house just because some slattern has started a rumor? I will accept it, Abram, but only long enough for everyone to see that you have not done this terrible thing they accuse you of. Then she must go elsewhere!"

Knowing that Sarah would never agree for me to go, Felix kindly offered to drive to Puzzle Creek and bring Nancy Hanks to Ocona Lufta as soon as he could, weather permitting.

I wrote to Nancy Hanks immediately, explaining the circumstances whereby she must return with Felix. Then I set about to do something that was equaled in difficulty only by my first declaration of guilt to Sarah. I wrote the complete truth of the situation to my beloved daughter Nancy, and implored her to come to Ocona Lufta and take Nancy Hanks back to Kentucky with her.

Sarah Enloe

I had long reconciled myself to our move but the aches, pains, and exhaustion incurred in settling into a new place kept me from praising our new cabin overmuch to Abram. Now we were here we would unpack and handle every object that we had brought with us and put them in exactly the same places that they had been in our old cabin. Now what kind of sense did that make? However, I was determined to make the best of it and as I looked around I could see that not only was the cabin judiciously sited and extremely well built, the surrounding land was rich and fine.

The children, even the older girls, were excited and found it difficult to concentrate on unpacking with so much new territory to explore. With her usual efficiency, Nancy Hanks worked steadily at whatever needed to be done. Nearly every evening she sat close by the fireplace sewing or mending.

"Goodness, Nancy Hanks! You'll ruin your eyes with so much sewing! What have you there anyway?"

She mumbled something about a ripped seam and after a few minutes, left the room. Well, she was tired like the rest of us. We'd all be more cheerful when we had some time to recover from the rigors of the long journey and getting settled.

Long before all of our unpacking was done, I yearned to be in my garden planting whatever I could. I would keep my vegetable seeds until next spring but the rhubarb, asparagus, and horseradish begged for the soil. Also, rooted apple and cherry cuttings needed to go into the ground so they would have time to settle in before winter. I had told Abram where I thought the springhouse should be and had chosen a level place for clothes drying poles. I was just beginning to reconcile myself to all this starting over when my world suddenly collapsed.

One evening just after supper, I needed Nancy Hanks for something and went in search of her. I came upon her suddenly on the back steps, a dark form silhouetted against the evening sun. She held her hands clasped in a way that pulled her thin dress against her lower belly. My breath caught in my throat. No! No, it could not be! Nancy Hanks with child? I was stunned to silence and then she looked up. She saw my expression and could tell that I understood. She lowered her eyes and stood mutely. I put my arm around her and walked her into the house. She refused to sit down and still did not speak, but soon began to shake with great convulsive sobs.

"Nancy, child, Nancy, don't take on so. We'll work it out. Whoever is the father, he must be made to marry you, we'll see to that."

Instead of taking comfort in my words, she sobbed even louder and I could sense a hysteria rising within her.

"Stay here," I said. "I'll get Abram."

As I crossed the yard I could still hear her sobs. Anger began to well up in me. Men...men!

I met Abram coming out of the barn and quickly gave him my story. Instead of looking surprised, his face went deathly pale and he slowly sat down on a large stump that served as a block for splitting kindling.

"Abram, what is it? What's wrong? Did you already know about this? And the father?"

"Sarah," he said. "Sarah, this is the most difficult thing I've ever had to do. I...I ask for your forgiveness and your understanding."

"What do you mean?" A tiny point of fear began to grow in my breast. "Abram, what do you mean?"

He raised his head and looked me straight in the eye.

"Nancy Hanks...the child is mine. Sarah, I'm the father of her child."

The world began to spin and darken but I fought to remain conscious. I felt Abram's hand on my shoulder but I struck it away. Words, I needed words but they would not come. Suddenly, a terrible nausea swept over my body in a sickening wave and I struggled to the corner of the barn and spilled my supper on the ground.

When I was able to breathe again I felt as if I was caught in some horrible delusion from which I could not escape. All the while, Abram stood like a marble statue, unmoving except for the tears that coursed down his face.

I stumbled toward the house, again shrugging off Abram's attempt to help. Nancy Hanks was gone, to her room, I supposed. I had to be alone so I slammed the bedroom door behind me and turned the latch before collapsing on our bed.

Our bed? Here? When? For how long? All questions and no answers. The remainder of the evening and then a sleepless night went by. At one point I vowed that I would go back to Puzzle Creek, to my family, then immediately I thought of countless reasons why that would be impossible.

I had no concept of time passing. Shock, rage, disappointment, self-pity, pain, all blended together until they became one great mass of unrelenting fury.

No one came to my door that night but now and then I sensed a presence outside. The sun was up when I came out to find Abram sitting on the floor, leaning back against the wall, arms and head resting on his knees.

I could speak now and say what I wanted but anger had rendered my body incapable of any other emotion except a morbid sort of curiosity.

"We have to talk, Abram. I want to hear it all, everything!"

He began to speak as soon as the parlor door closed. After a few minutes I thought of interrupting him, for the details I had demanded were almost too excruciating to hear. My mind seemed to speak to me and say that it was too much all at once. But, I thought, no, no, let it all be told now so there is no more to hear.

Finally Abram finished and stood as if waiting for my response. My God, what words could be expected from someone whose entire world had just fallen into ruins?

The silence was deadening. I could feel, almost hear, my heart pounding in my breast. Maybe, just maybe, this was all a ghastly dream from which I would awake and…then he spoke.

My body seemed to react on its own and I rushed at him wanting only to make him hurt as I was hurting. I pounded his chest with my fists until weakness forced me down into a chair. Abram remained silent and finally I wiped my eyes and looked up.

In words that were impossible to misinterpret I told him that she must leave, and now! He had the audacity to refer to the Biblical story of Hagar. My contempt for him at that moment was colossal. When I finished speaking, and what I said was plain and final, Abram left the parlor without another word.

For one brief moment, I considered letting Nancy Hanks leave without speaking to her. Then in the same way that I had wanted to make Abram share my agony, I knew I wanted her to feel it also. Why should she get by with causing such great pain and not partake of it herself? I sent Mary to her room with a message that I wanted to see her.

She sat before me stone-faced, her shoulders rigid, her hands clasped tightly, the bones of her knuckles showing white through the skin.

In a voice that I almost did not recognize, I told her that I knew everything, every detail, and I recounted many of them.

"While I was away from home, with my two small children in the house, you were coupling with my husband. While I was away from home and all but two of my children were in the house, you were in the barn with my husband. While I was ill and wishing you soon home, you lay on the ground with my husband. You have repaid my trust and generosity by deceiving me in the worst way possible. I could say much more but I will only declare that I hope soon never to look on your face again!"

Her face was devoid of any color except for her lips that had turned almost blue. She attempted to speak but all that I could hear were fragments.

"Sorry…I'm sorry. …never meant it to happen, never wanted to hurt…"

I left the room, fearful that I would allow myself to feel some misguided pity for her. My implacable anger was my only defense against emotional degeneration and I would not, could not let it slip away. The bedroom provided sanctuary against just such a happening. I did not see her again.

Nancy Hanks was gone by midday. Now our task was to approach the children with some feasible story. They were all very attached to her, the youngest five having known her all their lives. Our explanation would have been easier if we had treated her as a servant over the years but unfortunately we had not. Finally, I governed my feelings to some extent and was able to speak with Abram long enough to concoct a lie for the younger children, that Nancy Hanks had gone to keep house for the Walkers. We told a partial truth to Mary and Lizzie, that Nancy Hanks was with child, that she would not name the father, and that she had chosen to leave.

Slowly the days dragged by. Abram, in his usual way, plunged himself into his work, doing more and more of the physical labor that would normally be done by his hired workers or George and Moses. I busied myself with anything and everything from mending to baking to guiding George in building beds and furniture for the schoolroom.

We had lapsed into a sort of truce, Abram and I, where we could at least have a calm discussion on necessary things. For appearances sake, we slept in the same room, in the same bed, but there were still miles between us.

I had not allowed myself to think ahead far enough to wonder about Nancy Hanks' future. She was out of my sight and with the exception of James, Jane and Essie, her name was not mentioned in my hearing.

Then, one day we had a visitor, Lena Wallace, wife of the man who had given Abram so much grief on our journey. She was on her way home from a visit to Jonathon Creek. She had stayed with Hester Stoakley who was recovering from a difficult delivery. I had never liked Lena Wallace for she had a sly manner that seemed to always promise an unsavory bit of gossip, usually about someone far above her in station. Her head bobbed knowingly and her small eyes glittered as she told me of stopping to call on the

Walkers. I steadied myself for what I knew was coming.

"Breedin', is Nancy Hanks! Aye, breedin' she be, and takin' no pains to hide it neither! And they do say she refuses to name the father!"

She watched my face with her beady eyes, her intention being, I was sure, to gauge my reaction so she might have something new to add to her story when she told it again. My lack of expression silenced her chatter and I was greatly relieved when she went on her way.

"Abram!"

Weariness and pain were plain in his eyes as I told him in no uncertain terms that Nancy Hanks must be moved farther away. After all, Jonathon Creek was only a day's ride away and I knew in my heart that there would be others like Lena Wallace who would eagerly stop by to give me the latest, whether or not I wanted to hear it.

"I don't know or care where, but far away from here!"

Abram sent William Gwynn with a letter to Felix Walker and waited until he had an answer before he told me of his plan to return Nancy Hanks to Puzzle Creek. Although her presence and her situation would undoubtedly be known to many, my family and friends included, at least Lena Wallace would not be seeing her, for the journey back and forth to Puzzle Creek was far beyond her means.

Again, we began to return to some manner of peace after Felix saw Nancy Hanks settled at the Fords in Puzzle Creek. But it was not to last. Felix came without notice one day and he and Abram went riding around the farm. Upon their return, Abram told me of a rumor circulating among the community actually suggesting that he had murdered Nancy Hanks!

For the first time in a long time, I felt a pang of sympathy for him. Then he told me that Nancy Hanks would have to be brought back to Ocona Lufta in order to disprove the rumor.

My heart sank with pain that had only lately begun to lessen. I made it clear to Abram that I would tolerate her presence long enough to dispel the rumor and not one day longer. He immediately began a letter to Felix Walker, the only person he could depend upon, asking him to bring Nancy Hanks back to Ocona Lufta. Then he wrote to tell her to make ready for the trip. He offered to show me the letter but I refused to look at it. Then he began a letter to our daughter in Kentucky, an action of which I did not approve, but since I could not offer any other way out, I accepted that it might be the only path to a feasible resolution.

Harrodsburg, Kentucky
15 March 1804

Dear Father,
You may imagine with what acute distress I digested the contents of your letter. Arthur can attest to the fact that I was struck dumb for hours and read your words again and again in hope that I had somehow mistaken their meaning.
Even now I hardly know what to say. Try though I might, I cannot bring myself to condemn you for I know your character and know that you would not intentionally act to harm my mother, or for that matter, Nancy Hanks. Nor can I condemn Nancy Hanks for I know that she has no mendacity in her and has fallen into this dreadful situation through no fault of her own. I mourn for my mother and how this dreadful state of affairs must be grieving her. Great harm has obviously been done but there seems no fair way to calculate

where to lay the blame. As you can see, I am an aggregation of conflicting emotions and still hope that I may awake and find it all a very bad dream.

Of course, Father, we will make the journey to the Ocona Lufta and remove Nancy Hanks and her child to Kentucky with us. Arthur says we may leave here in time to arrive around the first of April if the wagon roads are in good condition.

I believe you and my mother were right in not revealing the full truth of the situation to Mary, Lizzie, and Meggie. Only more pain and suffering would come from their knowing the true father of Nancy Hanks' child.

With the utmost concern,
Nancy Enloe Thompson

Nancy Hanks

We arrived in Ocona Lufta to a fine cabin ready to move into just as Mrs. Enloe had requested. I was happy, for it meant a room, a place to escape from inquisitive eyes. Not that I suspected anyone of prying but something that had become a certainty on the journey gave me reason for great caution. I was with child. There was no longer any doubt. I feared it might be obvious to others and that fear dulled my already reticent nature

My heart leapt in panic when Mrs. Enloe chided me one evening for spending too much time at sewing. Little did she know that I was letting out seams in my own clothing in an attempt to keep my condition hidden, at least until I had the occasion to speak to Mr. Enloe alone.

I waited and watched for an opportunity but he was nearly always with one of his men or Moses and George when he worked outdoors. On no occasion was he alone inside the house for one or more of the children were always close by.

Near terror had set in by the time I chanced to find him alone, out of sight of the house setting posts for a corral. By the sound of his voice, I knew he saw the anguish on my face.

"Nancy...Nancy, what's wrong? What has happened?"

The words tumbled from my lips, incoherently, I thought. But I could tell from his face that he understood perfectly. I was weak, tired, and unsteady. Mr. Enloe held me against him and I heard him say in a voice barely discernible, "Oh God, my God, what have I wrought?"

He asked me to wait until he could tell Mrs. Enloe himself and he promised me that he would work it all out somehow. I tried to look hopeful but deep within a dark misgiving had begun to spread and cast its ominous shadow over my soul.

"Yes," I said. "Yes, I will wait."

Time passed slowly even with all the extra work of settling into a new place. My mind was greatly occupied with hiding my condition, especially when every bit of food that passed my lips was followed by a terrible attack of nausea. I had begun to find some excuse to leave the house after every meal.

After supper one evening, I stood alone on the back steps having just recovered from emptying my stomach. I wiped my face and smoothed my rumpled dress and in the process, caressed my growing belly, something I had begun to do frequently and unconsciously. At the very moment my hands came together beneath my belly, the kitchen door opened and Mrs. Enloe stepped out.

A tiny gasp escaped her lips and I saw the disbelief in her eyes. At that moment I could not have spoken if my life depended upon it. In fact, I made not a sound until she touched me, put her arm across my shoulder and led me into the house. It was as if an iron fist had gripped my insides and was shaking me.

She told me to wait while she went to find Mr. Enloe. If I could have willed myself to die at that moment, I would have done it gladly. Instead, I stumbled to my room and flung myself down on the floor. After a while my sobbing ceased and the cold light of truth began to take over. Now she knew, for I knew he would not lie to her.

I crawled onto my bed and lay there in an emotional stupor. Fear, dread, shame, pain. Then I heard running footsteps and a door slamming. I remained in my room until almost dark, then forced myself downstairs to see Jane and Essie to bed. I held them longer than usual when I hugged them goodnight for in my heart I knew it might be the last time.

I went to the kitchen to fill my water pitcher and found Mr. Enloe standing there as though he were lost. I assured him that Mrs. Enloe had learned of my condition quite by accident. He answered by nodding but he did not speak.

When sleep finally came that night, it was filled with the most hideous of nightmares. Uncle Richard stretched out his hands imploring me to pull him from the fire while flames grew closer and closer to his face. My hands were stuck fast to my belly and I could not break them loose. A horrible half-human creature with a terribly misshapen face nodded its head again and again as its unblinking eyes stared accusingly into mine. Then my hands were caught in a loom and the weaver ran the shuttle in and out through my fingers. A voice said, "We'll have to cut if off at the wrist to make it work." I twisted my head around and saw that the voice came from a woman whose face was covered with hideous sores. I shrank from her and tried to run but the threads held my hands. The woman wiped her face slowly with a blue kerchief. The sores disappeared and my mother stood before me, a dreadful enigmatic grin distorting her lips, pulling them back over yellow teeth.

I screamed over and over and awoke not knowing whether all the screams had come silently in my dream. Cold sweat soaked my body and my heart pounded fiercely. I dared not allow myself to sleep again for I was convinced that my dreams somehow foretold my future. If there was more I did not want to know it. I got up, wrapped my shaking body in a quilt and spent the remainder of the night in a chair.

At first light, I dressed and went downstairs. As I passed the narrow hall that led to the schoolroom and the Enloe's bedroom, I saw Mr. Enloe sitting on the floor, his back against the wall. I did not make my presence known and continued to the kitchen. I revived the fire and went about starting breakfast wondering with each movement if this would be the last time.

Neither Mr. nor Mrs. Enloe came to the kitchen for breakfast. After making sure the younger children had eaten, I went back to my room. The abnormal silence of the house was deafening and I knew not what to do except sit and wait. I answered a knock on my door to find Mr. Enloe standing there, his face a study in misery.

First he apologized for the situation he had created and when I tried to acknowledge my complicity, he said, "No, Nancy, let me at least be man enough to admit to the terrible wrong I've done. This would never have happened if I had governed my inclinations and not indulged my weakness."

He went on to tell me that I must leave right away and explained that William Gwynn would take me in the wagon to the Walkers. He held me in his arms briefly.

"Nancy, you know I never meant to hurt you. Don't ever forget that I have loved and will always love you."

Then he turned and left without waiting for me to answer.

All my belongings fitted into two canvas bags. I had just finished packing when Mary came to tell me that her mother wished to see me in the parlor immediately.

"Nancy Hanks," Mary said. "What's wrong with everyone this morning? Papa won't speak and Mama is very strange!"

I assured her that all would soon be well, belying my certainty that nothing would ever be well again.

Mrs. Enloe sat upright and stiff on the edge of her chair. She motioned for me to sit and I eased myself down to a place on a small sofa across from her.

My body felt as if it were made of stone, as if it would break apart if I moved too quickly. I clasped my hands together as tightly as I could and bit the inside of my lip hoping the pain would help me to maintain control.

Mrs. Enloe began to speak and in a voice cold and low, she told me that she knew everything, every detail of my illicit relationship with her husband. Every word, every sentence, cut through me like a knife.

One might think that when confronted with such truths, the face would burn with shame. The shame was there but my entire body was cold, cold as death. I tried to speak but my words came only in incoherent fragments.

Mrs. Enloe stood and stared at me for a moment, a strange expression on her tired face. Then she turned abruptly and without another word, left the room.

By midday William Gwynn had readied the wagon and loaded my two bags on the back. I said goodbye to the children with as normal a face as I could manage while avoiding their questions. Mr. Enloe helped me into the wagon but I turned my face away from him. I knew if I looked at him or spoke my meager control would weaken and I would break into tears. When I knew we were close to going out of sight, I turned and looked back. He stood watching. In my heart I waved goodbye to him but my hands were as heavy as lead and lay unmoving in my lap.

The weather was dry and the road in good condition. William Gwynn seemed not inclined to talk for which I was grateful. The landscape went by hour after hour as only a blur until along my side of a very narrow passage we came to the edge of a great ravine. It occurred to me how very easy it would be to throw myself from the wagon into the nothingness of death on the rocks below. Then the moment was past. Still, only emptiness lay ahead.

The Walker's welcomed me quietly. I had no way to know how much Mr. Enloe might have told them but I guessed that while Mrs. Walker knew of my condition, she did not know of Mr. Enloe's involvement. Since they had been generous enough to give me shelter, I felt I must make some effort to repay them. After resting for a day, I offered my assistance at mending or whatever tasks might need doing. Mrs. Walker appeared grateful for my offer.

"Yes, my dear," she said. "There's always lots of chores to do. But, the Enloes have frequently commended your help in the classroom. Would you mind spending some time with Ethan? His reading is quite atrocious and I can't seem to interest him in doing better."

Seven-year-old Ethan was not really a challenge. I had begun to help Nancy and Mr. Enloe with Joseph when he was of just such an age. Ethan was precocious and bright and I savored the hours I spent with him for only during that time was my mind ever away from my situation. Sewing, mending and ironing were mindless tasks that allowed my thoughts to wander to places dark and sinister.

I had been at the Walkers just over two weeks when Lena Wallace came to visit. She was not a well-liked woman but was tolerated because she had been a neighbor in Puzzle Creek. Her eyes seldom left me while she conversed with Mrs. Walker and I could almost hear the stories she would tell on her return to Ocona Lufta. Mrs. Walker was cordial but shortened the visit by telling Mrs. Wallace that she was very occupied with preparing for a visit from one of Mr. Walker's friends from Raleigh.

However comfortable the Walkers made my stay at their home, it was not to last. Mr. Walker handed me a letter one day that I could see immediately was from Mr. Enloe. Lena Wallace had stopped in at the Enloes and greatly disturbed Mrs. Enloe with her story of my obvious condition. Mrs. Enloe insisted that I must go further away so Mr. Walker was to take me back to Puzzle Creek.

I had never anticipated that I would stay with the Walkers indefinitely but I was sad to leave them, especially as I had no idea where I would go. Mr. Walker explained that Mr. Enloe had suggested that we ask the Tanners in Puzzle Creek to take me in since it had always been rumored that my father was a Tanner. The rumor might always have been around but it was a revelation to me. But what choice had I? By my actions I had placed myself into an untenable position and must now depend upon the charity of others.

Fortunately, the Walkers had already planned a trip to the Yadkin and could see me to Puzzle Creek with not much extra trouble. Mr. Walker had devised a conveyance that was part phaeton, part wagon that could make better time than a wagon but was infinitely more comfortable. He had created a collapsible cover that could be raised to keep out sun or rain. We arrived in late afternoon and went directly to the village tavern for a hot drink to stave off the chills of a damp mizzeling day. Then we drove to the Tanners. They lived in what was commonly called a dogtrot cabin that consisted of two large rooms joined by a roof that simply covered empty space. This kind of cabin was frequently built when two families lived together. Tanners lived on each side and both were at home when we arrived. They let us know in openly hostile language that I was not welcome and that they felt no responsibility for me. Although I had no idea of what lay ahead, I found myself rejoicing that they had rejected me.

Mrs. Walker patted my shoulder and said, "Don't be alarmed, Nancy. We have another option."

The next day we drove away from Puzzle Creek and after a short while, and to my great surprise, I realized that we were on the road to the Enloe's old home.

Mr. Walker then explained that Mr. Enloe had had a contingency plan. In case I was unwanted at the Tanners, I was to be delivered to his tenants, the Fords, with a letter making arrangements for them to give me shelter at his expense.

Upon arriving at the farm I felt very strange at being back in my old home that I had thought never to see again. Pleasant memories brought tears to my eyes.

Mr. Walker went inside for a while as we waited in the carriage. He returned accompanied by a middle-aged woman with a quiet sweet face. She welcomed me in a very pleasant manner and asked Mrs. Walker to come in for tea. In a very short time the Walkers were on their way to the Yadkin and I was again settling myself into new surroundings.

The Fords were kindly people and childless so the house was not nearly so full as it had been when the Enloes lived there. They gave me my old room and told me to make myself at home without any questions about my obvious condition. After settling in I informed Mrs. Ford that I was very efficient with the needle and almost every other household task and would be glad to help in any way I could. She smiled and thanked me.

In the coming weeks, my days were nowhere close to being full, even helping Mrs. Ford around the house. The few books I found, I read again and again. Occasionally I allowed myself to hope that I might hear from Mr. Enloe but I squelched the idea as quickly as it rose. To entertain that possibility was to set myself up for disappointment for I knew our bond was broken.

On a cold February morning I stood over the kitchen table ironing one of Mr. Ford's shirts. I set one iron back on the fireplace rack and picked up a heated one. As I turned toward the table a great wrenching pain almost threw me to the floor. My anguished cry brought Mrs. Ford running. She took one look at me and said, "It's time."

Until she spoke I had not even considered that my time would come. Indeed I had worked very diligently at not allowing myself to admit that that time would ever arrive, although I knew deep down that it was inevitable.

Mr. Ford sent one of his workers to Puzzle Creek and he returned with an elderly black midwife who took charge matter-of-factly and shooed Mrs. Ford out of the room. I remembered the mid-wife who had attended Mrs. Enloe and was grateful that she had not been brought for me.

The birth was not a difficult one. What pain I suffered disappeared when the mid-wife laid my son in my arms. Though my eyes were blurred with tears, I saw immediately the resemblance to his father. A shock of still-wet black hair, long gangly arms and legs, and a neck a little too thin for his head. Although I had heard that all newborns had the same color eyes, his were very dark and set deep beneath thick brows. Somehow he had a serious look about him, like a little old man. As he grew day by day I finally broke through my own sadness and tickled him under the chin until he gurgled and smiled. Then he returned quickly to what I came to think of as his old man's face.

I called him Abraham. Could I have given him any other name? The only thing that was certain about my future was that it would be a difficult one but at least I would have my child.

When little Abe was three weeks old, I awoke one morning aware that I had had a most remarkable dream. Unlike my nightmares of the past, I was in a field of beautiful flowers which I gathered until I had an armful. Suddenly a dark cloud appeared and there was a rumble of thunder. Then there were people all around me. I found myself in front of an elevated structure of pure gold and I walked forward and laid the flowers on it. At once the clouds parted and the sun shone from a clear blue sky. When I looked down, instead of the flowers, my child lay on the golden altar smiling up at me.

I did not know what the dream was meant to foretell, if anything, although I puzzled over it for days. Finally I decided to simply be glad that my child, my son, my Abraham was smiling.

Abraham was just one month old when a letter arrived from Mr. Enloe. With trembling hands I opened it carefully. The message was an incredible one and I read it several times to make sure I had not misunderstood.

My absence had invoked a rumor that had spread among the settlers in Ocona Lufta and Jonathon Creek that Mr. Enloe had "done away" with me! I was instructed to make ready for Felix Walker to take me back to Ocona Lufta where my presence would dispel the wicked rumor. Mr. Enloe went on to tell me that his daughter, my dear friend, Nancy Enloe Thompson, would be at his home when I arrived and would take me back to Kentucky with her. The word "you" obviously meant that he did not know that my child had been born. But how could he know? I had not dared to write to anyone in Ocona Lufta and had not even kept my promise to correspond with Mrs. Walker.

So I was once more to return to Mrs. Enloe's house, a prospect that was no more pleasant to me than I was sure it was to her. It was a sign of her regard for Mr. Enloe that she could bear to have me there, however briefly, to dispel a rumor that must be personally painful to him and disastrous to his reputation as a fair and honest magistrate.

Since I had no exact date for when to expect Mr. Walker, I made ready as best I could and awaited his arrival. I took to sitting in the kitchen by the window where I could see the road. Little Abe's cradle sat beside me and I busied myself with sewing or mending. One morning I watched a man come riding down the road but I knew immediately that he was not Mr. Walker for he would be driving his carriage. My curiosity was aroused for his mount was a fine, tall gray horse. As he drew near the house I could see that he was a well-dressed handsome man but since his arrival had nothing to do with me, I sighed, rocked Abe's cradle with my foot, and went back to my mending.

I heard his knock on the front door and Mrs. Ford as she spoke to him. I was astounded when she came to the kitchen and said that the stranger had asked to see me and was waiting in the parlor.

My earlier impression of him was correct. He was a very fine-looking man and took my hand in a most genteel way. He introduced himself as Michael Tanner of Virginia and forthrightly informed me that he was my father!

I had labored for so long to keep my emotions in check that I must have seemed cold and unfeeling in my lack of response. He proceeded to tell me of his family, his involvement with my mother, and how I had come to live with my Uncle Richard.

He offered to help me in any way he could and pressed me to accompany him back to Virginia. I marveled that this man from such a prominent family would be willing to risk his reputation for me.

I declined his offer but he seemed so easy to confide in that I relayed the whole story about how I had come to be in this position. Also, I told him my apprehension about whether I had possibly inherited some moral disease from my mother. He shook his head and told me that whatever my misfortunes had been he could believe no evil of me.

Finally, since I would not agree to any of his other offers, he insisted on hiring a wagon and driving me back to Ocona Lufta. I agreed for I was weary with waiting and knew we would likely meet Mr. Walker somewhere along the way. Early in the morning, two days later, we left for Ocona Lufta.

Michael Tanner

I had not been to North Carolina for seventeen years and would not now be on my way except that a letter had arrived from my brother in Richmond some weeks before to tell me of his serious illness. During my visit with Daniel, he gave me an account of a long ago circumstance that concerned us both and soon after being assured that he was on the mend, I headed south.

Our grandparents had come to Virginia from Germany in the early 1700's with wealth enough to purchase property and begin life in the new world in a manner far above most immigrants of the day. Daniel and I grew to manhood in a privileged environment but accepting the responsibilities incumbent upon us in our station, including good educations.

Daniel was the serious one and, by the age of twenty, had settled down to married life with the daughter of a neighboring planter. I was the personable one, so it was said, conscientious and dependable in every way except where the opposite sex was concerned. Regarded as handsome, I had inherited my mother's dark hair and eyes, and could have had my choice of the neighborhood girls. Instead, I became entangled with a young, voluptuous wench, an itinerant weaver who spent time in the area each fall weaving cloth from the cotton, wool, and flax grown on the surrounding plantations. Her name was Lucy Hanks and she gave birth to a daughter in 1784 and named her Nancy. Much to my family's chagrin, I installed Lucy and her baby in a small cottage in a village on the far side of our plantation and helped her along with gifts of money and food. Ten months passed and Lucy's wanderlust overcame her motherly concerns and what little affection she had for me. She left the baby with a neighbor and went her own way, and as far as I ever knew, never returned to that particular area of Virginia.

I was greatly affected, not because Lucy was gone, but because I felt a great responsibility for the child who I believed to be my own. It so happened that my brother and his wife had tried in vain to conceive and had eventually resigned themselves to remaining childless. I convinced Daniel and his wife to take Nancy and bring her up as their own, promising them that she would never know that they were not her true parents unless they chose to tell her. The situation seemed ideally settled until Daniel's wife died suddenly a year later. He remarried within the year and upon finding out that two-year-old Nancy was both baseborn and not Daniel's child, his second wife declared that she would not have her in the house. I was away on family business in England at the time so Nancy was taken to the next county over and left with her nearest known relative, her mother's brother, Richard Hanks.

Upon my return a year later, I learned that Richard Hanks, along with some Tanner cousins and other folk had left Virginia to seek land of their own in Rutherford County in North Carolina. By the time I was able to make the trip, Dicky Hanks, as he was called, had built a cabin and seemed well settled. The child, having not seen me for nearly two years did not recognize me and seemed to be happy with her uncle and his already substantial family. I gave him some money and left her to be raised by him and his wife. My slight guilt at leaving her was tempered by the fact that I was soon to be married myself. I strongly suspected that my fiancée, the honorable Miss Carter, would not react sympathetically to the open acknowledgement of a natural daughter. Time moved on and with a family of my own, memories of the child faded somewhat, but never entirely expired. I gave thought sometimes to trying to find her but always suppressed the notion by declaring that she was likely better off wherever she was than if interfered with by a stranger.

Then came the letter from Richmond and Daniel's revelation that Nancy had remained in North Carolina with her uncle until she was around ten years old and had then been sold as a bondservant by her mother.

As soon as I could arrange the trip, I left for North Carolina and upon my arrival found that Richard Hanks had been dead for several years, the victim of a house fire. As I traveled about the community seeking the whereabouts of the child, I remembered that some Tanner cousins had settled there also. Upon locating them, I could see that they had not progressed a great deal beyond what their status had been in Virginia. When I inquired about Nancy, one of them smirked knowingly and proceeded to tell me with revolting eagerness the circumstances of her present situation. I obtained directions to where she was living but I almost turned back toward Virginia on the premise that I had no business interjecting myself into such a dubious state of affairs when it was not by any means certain that the young woman was actually my daughter.

However, I could not leave. I followed the well-traveled wagon road out of Puzzle Creek and soon reached a large and prosperous looking farm. There seemed to be no one about except some workers in a distant field so I rode up to the house, dismounted and knocked on the door. I had raised my hand to knock a second time when a middle-aged woman in a dust cap opened the door. I removed my hat and asked her if there was a young woman there by the name of Nancy Hanks. A faint look of surprise showed on her face, and then she quietly asked me inside and showed me to a parlor where she indicated I was welcome to sit down. After a few minutes a young woman came into the room.

I did not need to question her. I knew immediately that she was my daughter for she was the very image of a portrait of my mother that had been painted at just that age. Her forehead was high and crowned with thick black hair; her eyes were dark gray, large and steady. She was modestly but tastefully dressed and carried herself with a deportment that told of a good upbringing.

Perhaps she sensed something familiar in me also for she was calm and showed little emotion when I told her my name and that I was her father. I said that I had heard something of her predicament and had come at this late date to offer my services in any way that I could be of assistance to her and the child.

How long we sat in the parlor I do not know but soon we quitted the house and walked outside. We found a sturdy bench near the vegetable garden and sat down. I told her my story from the beginning and how I came to be there at this time. She listened quietly, seldom interjecting any comment into my story. When finally I had finished, she spoke.

"I don't remember you precisely but sometimes over the years I have had a faint recollection of a person of your stature and coloring who spoke kindly to me. Perhaps it was when you came to Uncle Richard's. Anyway, I thank you for coming now."

She proceeded to tell me the story of her life since the day her mother had left her with the Enloe family. I felt a sharp anger well up in me toward Abram Enloe but she spoke so kindly of him that I could not give it voice. Then she began to speak of Lucy Hanks.

"Sometimes," she said, "I wonder if I am destined to be like her, if in the same way my sister Mandy inherited her talent for weaving, my mother passed on to me a moral disease, an inclination toward wickedness so deep that it will never go away. You see, I cannot feel that my association with Mr. Enloe is morally wrong and consequently by that very feeling, I must be depraved. I have tried to make myself believe that our union is wanton and corrupt but I cannot persuade myself. So you see, I am lost and there is no way for me to atone without the added vice of hypocrisy. But, I am most unhappy for the pain I have caused to people as dear to me as any natural relations could be, God knows I am."

Sadly, I could not respond to her speech for its meaning tore at my heart. So instead I asked to see the letter from Mr. Enloe. After reading it I said, "How can I assist you? Shall you go back to Virginia with me? Say what you will and I am resolved to make it happen."

She would not even entertain the idea of going to Virginia. Indeed, the only assistance to which she would consent was that I escort her and the infant back to the Enloes so she would not have to linger for the arrival of Mr. Walker.

I hired a light wagon and we left early in the morning two days later.

Chapter Six

Abram Enloe

How relieved I was to receive our Nancy's letter and hear that she did not see fit to condemn but instead, offered her assistance. She and Arthur arrived as she had hoped on the first of April. How simultaneously comforting and painful to welcome her to our new home under such circumstances. Of course, Arthur knew our situation in detail but could not have conducted himself in a more tactful and understanding manner.

I tried to accept their presence as a simple visit but the precise reason hung over us like a thundercloud. Although our Nancy and I spent time alone riding around the farm and assessing the horses, she never openly spoke of Nancy Hanks except to assure me that she would see her settled in Kentucky as well as she could. She had learned that Lucy Hank's sister lived near Harrodsburg and was married to a respectable man named Richard Berry. They had agreed to share their home with Nancy Hanks and our Nancy had assured them that some compensation would be provided for their trouble.

Our Nancy and Arthur had been at our home for five days when one of the children spotted Felix Walker's carriage. I could not stop my heart from pounding in anticipation of seeing Nancy Hanks again. Sarah was nowhere to be seen but everyone else congregated in the front yard to greet the carriage.

Our Nancy was the first to step forward and greet Nancy Hanks. Then the younger children swarmed around her. My attempt to remain calm and detached was almost thwarted when Nancy Hanks stepped through the mob with a baby in her arms. How ridiculous of me not to have anticipated that image.

I greeted her but did not extend my hand or acknowledge the child. She met my eyes only briefly but in that fleeting moment I knew that her feelings for me had not changed. As old memories swept over me, I reminded myself that this was dangerous ground I was treading. I would have to guard against any action that would erode the progress I had made in mending my fences with Sarah. But, how difficult it was to project this detached countenance to Nancy Hanks while my heart beat wildly at the very sight of her.

That afternoon and evening everyone was ill at ease. After Sarah finally appeared there was much talk about the most trivial of matters. Mary chatted nervously about a new style of sleeve that had been described to her in a letter from a Puzzle Creek friend.

Our Nancy spoke at great length of the large numbers of settlers that were coming to or going through Kentucky. Sarah did not speak except as necessary during supper. Shortly after, she excused herself and left the room.

After everyone else had retired, I climbed the stairs to say goodnight to Essie and Jane, something their mother normally did. Perhaps I knew that Nancy Hanks was to share their room but still I was startled to see her there. She sat in a low wooden rocker, the child asleep in her arms. His appearance was very familiar to me for he could have been either of my other sons at that age. I felt like a tongue-tied boy and simply spoke the first words that came to mind.

"So, what name have you given him, Nancy Hanks?"

She looked up at me through gentle gray eyes and said, "Why, Abraham, of course."

I left the room without another word. I could deal with unruly horses, courtroom brawls, wild animals and hard physical labor but I could not cope with this violent emotion that threatened to overpower me.

It had been settled that our Nancy and Arthur would leave the morning after Nancy Hanks arrived. Early the next day we all assembled in the front yard as we had done the day before. I helped Arthur load Nancy Hanks' bags and the baby's cradle in the back of the wagon. Then our Nancy climbed up to her seat and reached down to take the baby from its mother's arms. Behind me, I heard Sarah catch her breath but I did not turn around. It was all I could do to control my own emotion without making an attempt to console her that might well be rejected.

After the wagon rolled away I turned to see Sarah with a peculiar mix of pain and pleasure on her face. I did not speak and headed for the barn. Before I was out of earshot, I heard James say, "But I wanted Nancy Hanks to stay this time!"

Although her words were not distinct, the acrimony in Sarah's voice was very clear.

Everything I could do, under the circumstances, I had done to appease my wife and detach myself from any further involvement with Nancy Hanks. I had not been able to directly offer her anything but when I helped Arthur lift the cradle into the wagon, I slipped a small deerskin bag filled with coins and the only copy of her bondservant agreement beneath the blankets. At least she would not enter Kentucky as a penniless servant. I had also given our Nancy a generous sum and asked her to pay the Berrys a certain amount each month for giving shelter to Nancy Hanks and her child. To my silent entreaty, our Nancy answered, "No, Father. I will not tell my mother about this. It would serve no purpose."

Felix Walker, William Gwynn and several other people from nearby homesteads could now attest that Nancy Hanks was alive and well. I struggled to suppress the anger and disappointment I still felt about the rumor that had been spread. I had always endeavored to be fair with my fellowman whether in or out of court and had settled many cases to the mutual advantage of both parties. I had always known that a certain amount of jealousy existed among some members of the community, mostly because I had begun wilderness life with property and had surpassed most of them in my undertakings.

To resent me for my success on the farm was as absurd as if the parties concerned had taken exception to the number of children I had sired.

When I informed Sarah that I had decided to resign from my magisterial appointment, she protested at first for she had enjoyed the community standing the position had given her. Then she conceded that my moral dilemma had definitely undermined my civil authority. I could read her well enough to see that she would have liked to openly blame Nancy Hanks but she had also learned to do some suppressing of her own in the name of peace and quiet.

I had never been a drinking man, only the odd pint of hard cider or a nip of good rum on occasion. So as usual I tried to dull my senses with hard work. But still I was subject to total despair when unwanted memories encroached and I was forced to ask myself if I could ever atone for my transgressions.

Sarah Enloe

Our Nancy and Arthur arrived as they had hoped, on the first of April. I could readily see that she was well and happy. She had matured and when we talked it was more as equals than as mother and daughter. I suppressed my desire to raise the name of Nancy Hanks for I knew her fondness for the girl and knew also that I had nothing good to say about her. So we talked of gardens and cooking and sewing. She marveled at how much her brothers and sisters had grown in her absence and how large and comfortable our new home was. She asked for rhubarb, asparagus, and horseradish roots and summoned Arthur to inspect our cellar and springhouse but she never mentioned Nancy Hanks.

I did not go out front when the Walkers and their passenger arrived but watched from the window while the children swarmed around her. I will admit it pained me to see Mary and Lizzie competing to see who would first hold Nancy Hanks' bastard. My revulsion was diminished somewhat by the sheer fact that she would soon be gone. Surely, I thought, we can no longer be held responsible after she has gone so far away!

I had not welcomed Nancy Hanks but I was happy to add my silent farewell to the others the next morning. I stayed quiet through it all until I saw her hand her baby up to our Nancy who had already boarded the wagon. The child's blanket fell away exposing its long arms and legs and a shock of thick black hair. I gasped in dismay at the child's obvious resemblance to my husband. Adam was standing in front of me and if he heard me, he did not react. I turned my back in order to hide my distress from the others. After the wagon rolled away, Abram walked toward the barn without speaking.

Later that day Abram informed me that he would give up his position as magistrate. I knew it pained him terribly to do so for he had always been praised as a fair and just mediator who tried his best to settle every case with as little trouble and expense as possible to all parties concerned. But I agreed that the rumor had damaged his credibility. I did not speak what was in my mind, that Nancy Hanks was at fault, for I had agreed to hold up my side of our bargain to try to reconcile our differences.

Nancy Hanks was gone and pray God she would stay gone this time. I almost wished her luck but I had not that much charity left in me.

Nancy Hanks

"My father," I thought. "What a grand sound that has!"

What a pleasant surprise to learn that I had such a father as Michael Tanner. What a great joy it was to me to know that one of my parents was intelligent, educated, responsible and moral. Somehow it made me feel less convinced that I had inherited a depraved disposition from my mother.

On the trip toward Ocona Lufta, Michael Tanner told me long stories of his boyhood in Amelia County, Virginia and described his family to me. Influenza had taken his wife after eleven years of marriage and along with her their two young sons. His brother David lived in Richmond and had very little to do with managing the family plantation. Their mother had been dead for many years and their father was elderly and infirm.

As we moved further toward Asheville, I believe my father maintained some hope that I would change my mind and go to Virginia with him. Perhaps I would regret my decision sometime in the future but I was determined not to be the cause of humiliation and pain to anyone else. Too many people knew of my circumstances and that knowledge would follow me to Virginia where it would heap scorn on someone who had done nothing to deserve it.

Abraham was a good child and gave little trouble on the journey. We traveled steadily and having no one to concern us except ourselves, made very good time. We met few people on the road, mostly men on horseback or empty freight wagons returning from Asheville or the Watauga Settlements. One morning we had barely crossed the Broad River beyond Asheville when I recognized Felix and Phoebe Walker approaching in their carriage. After introductions, we decided that we would return to Asheville so Mrs. Walker could purchase needed supplies. At Morrison's store, Michael Tanner urged me to choose something he could buy for little Abe and me. I accepted, for while I knew I would not change my mind, I did not want to seem ungrateful for his offer to give me a home nor for his assistance on the trip. So I chose a length of soft cloth that would make excellent gowns for the baby and another length that would make plain but sturdy dresses for me, plus a small decorated sewing box with scissors, needles, thimbles and an assortment of thread.

Our parting was poignant. Michael Tanner kissed me on the forehead and then held my hands against his lips. He patted little Abe's cheek and before he turned away, pressed a small leather purse into my hand. He walked away quickly before I could protest, boarded his wagon and rolled away.

The Walkers were much impressed with Michael Tanner. Mrs. Walker frowned and expressed concern when I told her that I had turned down his offer to share his Virginia home with me although I believe she understood my reasoning.

We arrived at the Enloe's Ocona Lufta home and were met by Nancy and Mr. Thompson, and Mr. Enloe's whole family except for his wife. Several other people were there and I suspected their presence was to document my state of mortality.

What a joy to see my dear friend once again and find that she was not changed in her feelings for me and, indeed, clasped me and my child in a warm hug. Then we were inundated by the children who tried to greet me and look at little Abe at the same time. When they were satisfied, I moved forward and there was Mr. Enloe. He looked tired and weary but his eyes were the same as always. He spoke to me, then stared down at my child, his child, for a few seconds before walking over to help Mr. Walker unload my bags and little Abe's cradle from the carriage.

I had resolved that I would neither through speech nor deed do anything to disrupt the Enloe household. So I spoke only when spoken to. At the supper table, I accepted whatever was passed to me and asked for nothing. Mrs. Enloe spoke very little and was first to leave the table.

Nancy had told me that I would share Jane and Essie's bedroom and I had just finished feeding my baby and was rocking him to sleep when Mr. Enloe walked in. He seemed surprised at finding me there and immediately took a long quiet look at little Abe.

"So, what name have you given him?"

"Why, Abraham, of course."

Only a few times had I ever seen Mr. Enloe show such open emotion. He seemed to want to speak but he did not. He left without a word and I did not see him again until I was ready to board the Thompson's wagon the next morning.

Again, all the family, this time including Mrs. Enloe, were out front to see us off. I stood holding little Abe as the children said goodbye to their sister. She boarded the wagon and took the baby on her lap until I could climb on. Little Abe's covers fell away and I heard Mrs. Enloe gasp. When I turned to look her back was to us, an action so deliberate her message could not be mistaken. I boarded the wagon and for the first time since she learned that I was with child, I realized that I felt no sympathy for her. No matter her situation or her damaged relationship with her husband, she had him, her children, her home, security and standing among her contemporaries. I had only my son and soon I must determine how I would make a life for him. Although the occurrence was more infrequent than in the past, the courts still had the authority to remove a baseborn child from its mother and place it to be raised as a bondservant until the age of eighteen to twenty-one years. I would not have my son placed in such a position and as soon as I reached Kentucky I intended to use whatever qualities I had to insure that it never happened.

Our trip was pleasant with Nancy and me having time to reminisce about our past, at least up to a certain point. She never pressed me to talk about her father, choosing instead to speak of the future.

Little Abe and I stayed several nights with the Thompsons before moving in with my mother's sister Pearl and her husband, Richard Berry, who were childless. Pearl did not resemble anything I remembered of my mother. Indeed, she barely recalled her sister Lucy, for there was eleven years difference in their ages, my mother being the elder. They welcomed me into their home and gave me a small room that suited me very well. Nancy had told me that her father had provided money to compensate my uncle and aunt for our bed and board. Nevertheless, I made myself useful from the first day for I had no intention of disrupting my baby's and my life with another move any sooner than necessary.

Harrodsburg, Kentucky
10 September 1804

Dear Father,
Although our visit to Ocona Lufta was not under the best of circumstances, I was very glad to see everyone and Arthur was pleased to meet the rest of the family. Your new home is lovely and will serve as a model that Arthur and I may aspire to.
Father, your conversation with Arthur about combining your talents, experience and resources to build a mill and forge here in Harrodsburg has him in absolute bliss. I hope you will not change your mind for he is already evaluating suitable locations on our property for both endeavors. I am certain that you and Arthur would make admirable partners in such an enterprise.
Mother, so taken was Arthur with your springhouse and cellar that he vows to complete one of each for us as soon as possible. Of course, there will

be little to store in the cellar at this time of year but at least it will be ready for whatever we can manage to preserve next summer.

I do not see Nancy Hanks every day but apparently she and her child appear to be in good health. A neighbor of the Berrys has told me that Nancy Hanks has attracted the attention of a young man who aspires to be a schoolmaster and also a newcomer named Thomas Lincoln. I hope this mention of Nancy Hanks is not too painful but I thought both of you would be glad to know that she seems to be settling in very well.

Father, remember that we anxiously anticipate your presence in the spring.

Your loving daughter,

Nancy Enloe Thompson

Chapter Seven

Abram Enloe

The remainder of the year after Nancy Hanks went to Kentucky will always remain a blur to me. I worked in my normal frenzied fashion as I had always done when my mind was restless, but this time with little enthusiasm. While she was in Puzzle Creek or at Felix's, she had not seemed so far away. I knew the places and could picture her there but Kentucky was a blank to me.

Spring crops had been planted and most of my mares had foaled when I began to think about our Nancy's last letter and her entreaty for my presence in Harrodsburg to assist Arthur in building a gristmill and forge. I also remembered Sarah's response to the news that Nancy Hanks had begun walking out with someone.

"Well, the best thing that could happen for everyone is for her to marry!"

With those words in mind, I began gradually planting the seeds for a trip to Kentucky. I had thought long and hard on the idea of my son, Nancy Hanks' son, growing up branded as a bastard. I could not abide the idea and resolved that I would rather he bear some other man's name than endure the trials that the world would heap upon him as an illegitimate offspring.

At first Sarah objected, but when I told her my plans to pay someone to marry Nancy Hanks, she agreed, saying that she would never rest easy until the girl was settled in a permanent way. She would have liked to go to Kentucky to visit our Nancy but with ten children to consider and one of them a mere babe the notion was impossible. And she admitted she would not like to see Nancy Hanks again.

I left for Harrodsburg with the promise that I would make haste on the journey and in my assistance to our son-in-law. Sarah seemed reluctant to see me go but I told myself that she would not be quite so sorry to see me leaving for Augusta or Charleston or the Yadkin where there was no Nancy Hanks.

I found our Nancy and Arthur well situated in a cozy cabin near a goodly stream with enough force to turn a large waterwheel. Also, their location was near enough to the main road to support a small forge. Arthur had waited for my approval before making a final decision about locations but I could see that he had done a fine job on his own. After a few days of directing him and his helpers on getting started, I decided it was time for me to see Nancy Hanks.

Our Nancy had pointed out the Berry's place when she and Arthur took me for a ride to see some of the surrounding countryside. The Berry's cabin was well built and larger than I had expected. I wanted to see Nancy Hanks alone so I rode to a small group of trees not far from the cabin and waited until Mr. and Mrs. Berry left in their wagon.

My heart pounding like a schoolboy, I approached the cabin and knocked on the door. Nancy Hanks' face went white and I realized that she had no notion that I was in Kentucky. I had simply assumed that our Nancy had informed her of my presence. After recovering herself somewhat, she asked me in but seemed at a loss for any further words. To try and put her at ease, I began to speak about building the forge and mill, and then stopped almost involuntarily to tell her how fine she looked. She was no longer a girl but a woman with a woman's assurance about her. She accepted my compliment but still seemed puzzled at my presence.

When I began to explain, a bit of sadness crept into her expression.

"So, you've come to marry me off," she said. "To try and buy me a husband. Was that Mrs. Enloe's idea?"

In a voice I could barely control, I assured her that the idea was not only that she have someone to care for her but that her son not be raised in circumstances detrimental to his future. She seemed to understand and asked if I would like to see the child. She led me through a door into a room with a low ceiling that was obviously a later addition to the cabin. Her bed, a wooden rocker, and a small round table with one straight back chair left only enough room for a child's bed, for he had outgrown his cradle. We stood side by side and looked down at our sleeping son. Scarcely a year had passed and he looked even more like my other sons than he had as an infant. I turned away, my heart and soul racked with pain. How could it be that I was calmly making plans to resolve the future of my beloved and my son in such a way that I could never again claim them as my own?

Nancy Hanks felt my distress and laid her hand on my arm. I groaned and with both arms pulled her to me. There was no resistance on her part and we sank down on her bed. Afterward, we lay quietly and contented in each other's arms until the child stirred and brought us back to reality.

While she held little Abe on her lap, we returned to the subject of marriage. I pressed her to tell me if the young schoolmaster or the Lincoln fellow had proposed marriage to her.

"It's all I can do for you, Nancy. God help me, I would do differently if I could but you know why I can't."

With her old familiar composure she acknowledged that I could not reasonably do more than to see that she was married and that our son had a legal father. She finally agreed for me to speak with the schoolmaster and Lincoln and I asked her to do nothing until she heard from me. I returned to our Nancy's with the weight of the mission heavy on my heart. Nancy could not help but notice but in typical fashion she did not question me.

The moment I met Floyd Draper, I knew I did not want Nancy Hanks to marry him. He was young, maybe half my age and while not exactly handsome, I could see that he was the kind of man that aged well. Sandy hair swept over a high forehead above intelligent blue eyes. He was soft spoken, well-educated and hoped to organize a school in the settlement as soon a meeting place was built. He seemed to have no notion of my reason for seeking him out, apparently thinking me someone simply interested in education.

I contemplated the many reasons why Nancy Hanks should not marry Floyd Draper. Too young, not settled, no real profession or skills, not experienced enough in the ways of the world to embark on life in the wilderness with a ready-made family. No, he was just not suitable!

The next day I found Thomas Lincoln at the only tavern in the village. He was a short, stocky man. His fingers, which were wrapped around a beaker of ale, were wide and fleshy and covered with hair between the second knuckle and his hand. He slouched in his chair, his left arm dangling carelessly. His clothes were those of someone above his station but they were soiled from constant wear. I felt an immediate aversion to him but I did not let that stand in the way of asking him if he had proposed to Nancy Hanks. He bristled at first and asked me what business it was of mine to inquire into his personal affairs.

I explained that Nancy Hanks was a friend of my family and it was our wish that she be married for her own security and to give her child a name. A slight sneer told me that he suspected the truth of the situation.

He put down the beaker and with a stiff forefinger he prodded the table.

"So what are you telling me this for?"

I started to explain, realizing that I liked him less as each moment passed. He jabbed the same forefinger at me, almost touching my chest.

"So, what's in it for me?" he asked, jerking his thick thumb toward himself. "What would I get out of it?"

He seemed about to quit the conversation until I mentioned that I was prepared to settle five hundred dollars and a wagon and two horses on whomever she married.

He straightened his sagging shoulders and, although his mouth smiled, his eyes had no more warmth than a piece of slate.

"Now, that sure sweetens the pot," he said.

With a growing sense of disgust I laid out the details. We hoped Nancy Hanks would be married in less than six months and as soon as the event occurred, her husband could obtain the wagon, horses and cash at my daughter's home in Harrodsburg.

"But," I said, "if you are to be the man, I must have your promise right now that Nancy Hanks and her son will be provided a decent place to live and be well cared for. Otherwise I will look elsewhere."

Thomas Lincoln gave his promise readily which should have lessened my apprehension but I felt a great foreboding in my heart. However, I fought against the sensation and told myself that at last there was some hope that a situation that had seemed impossible might now be finally resolved.

I saw Nancy Hanks only once more while I was in Kentucky when one of our Nancy's neighbors hosted a small gathering. She came with the Berrys to whom she introduced me as her friend Nancy's father. A while later I spoke with her briefly and told her of my conversation with Thomas Lincoln. Her eyes widened slightly.

"But, what of Floyd Draper? I thought..."

When I finished telling her why Thomas Lincoln was to be preferred over Floyd Draper, my stomach was unsettled. I believe she understood my true reasoning only too well and it tore at my heart.

She almost shrugged and said, "Well, it doesn't matter now anyway. Floyd Draper has gone and no one seems to know where or why."

We spoke only a few more words and they were our final ones. I left for home a few days later and had been on the road two days before I allowed myself to admit what I had done. I dismounted and threw myself on the ground like a child.

"May God forgive me..." I said over and over through my tears. I had doomed Nancy Hanks to life with a crude, uneducated man of questionable morals when she could have wed someone far, far better. And I had done it because I could not bear the comparison of her memories of me to Floyd Draper, a man half my age, and both handsome and intelligent.

"May God forgive me."

Nancy Hanks

Time seemed to move slowly in Kentucky. I stayed busy but still the days lagged. I longed for at least a hint of what the coming years were to bring but nothing was revealed to me. As far as I could see in my future, my life was one unchanging series of days and weeks and months adding up to empty years. I tried to avoid dwelling on the past and that was why a letter from my sister Mandy, whom I had not seen for nearly nine years, was such a surprise. The tone of her letter was impersonal but I thought, how could it be otherwise? We were sisters only by virtue of having been borne by the same mother and had grown up strangers to each other. Mandy had met and married a young man named Samuel Henson and they were moving across the mountains. I suppose she wrote to me as her only known relative. The melancholy I felt on reading her letter was puzzling at first. Then I realized that my sadness came from not knowing her well enough to sincerely lament her leaving.

I filled my days with whatever chores Aunt Pearl gave me and I sewed. With the cloth my father had bought for me in Asheville, I made dresses for myself, and gowns for my child. I spent little of the money given me by my father and Mr. Enloe. Harrodsburg was not yet a true village and had only a small trading post filled mostly with tools and hunting supplies.

I had little opportunity to make acquaintances for my aunt and uncle did not socialize with many of their neighbors. Then one day a young man came to call, taking me quite by surprise for we had never met. His name was Floyd Draper and he hoped one day to start a school in Harrodsburg. Nancy Thompson had suggested he call on me but I could never settle on just what specifics he wished to discuss. My education far exceeded his in both depth and content. The only area where he was superior to me was in numbers, which I had never found interesting.

Floyd continued to call and I walked out with him, but always with little Abe in my arms. I had determined long before that any man interested in me would have to show the same consideration for my son. After a while, although I could not put my finger on it, I felt that I could never do more than like Floyd Draper, even though I knew many successful marriages had been based on much less than true love. Then one day I understood in a flash. I had been subconsciously weighing him against Mr. Enloe and Floyd came off as a weak and ineffectual youth in comparison.

Another person's acquaintance I made quite by accident. I was hanging wet sheets on the bushes in the back yard one sunny day when little Abe began to scream at the top of his lungs from where I had placed him on a blanket on the grass.

I started toward him so quickly that the sheet I was holding became entangled in my feet and I fell face down to the ground. I half arose on my own and then a man was helping me up. I shrugged him off and ran toward my child who continued to scream. I could see the cause immediately.

A bee had stung him on the upper arm and a large whelp had already risen. As I picked him up and began to comfort him, the person behind me said, "Here, let me put something on that."

He was a man I had seen only from a distance who sometimes worked with my uncle. He took a snuffbox from his pocket, opened it and removed a pinch between his finger and thumb. He sprinkled the powder into his palm and moistened it with a few drops of water from a rain barrel. Then he smeared a small amount of the paste over the tiny sting hole. In only a few minutes little Abe had stopped crying.

"Thank you," I said. "I wouldn't have known what to do."

He told me his name and that he worked with my uncle. I sensed that he wanted to talk further but I was interested only in getting my child indoors.

Thomas Lincoln did not pressure me but I sensed that he would be coming around again. And he did. He began to stop off at the cabin when he and Uncle Berry had finished their day's work. He never said so openly but he made it clear in other ways that he was there to see me. I walked out with him a few times but, as with Floyd Draper, took my child along.

I learned that Thomas Lincoln was uneducated but was experienced at many kinds of work. He was persistent in his attentions to me but I kept him at bay for there was a lot I did not know about him and I sensed that much of it might not be good.

I had not seen Nancy Thompson for several weeks, the distance to her place being too far to walk. My uncle's only conveyance was a heavy freight wagon that he nearly always employed in his work. The only time the wagon was used otherwise was when he took Aunt Pearl to visit friends who live north of Harrodsburg.

It was after my uncle and aunt had left on one of these Saturday visits that I answered the door and was rendered speechless.

Mr. Enloe stood there and for a moment I thought I might be dreaming. Then I recovered myself enough to ask him in. As if to put me at ease, he began to tell me about the mill and forge that he planned to build on his son-in-law's property.

Then he stopped in mid-sentence and told me that I was even lovelier than he remembered. They were sweet words but I knew that he had not come just to offer his compliments. My heart sank when he began to explain.

"So you've come to marry me off," I said, "to buy me a husband. Was that Mrs. Enloe's idea?

Honest as ever, he admitted, "Partly, yes. But, couldn't you consider it a dowry of sorts?"

However I felt, I understood his motivation. That my son not grow up without a legal father was a subject to which I had given much thought.

"Would you like to see him?" I asked.

Mr. Enloe nodded and I showed him to our room. He looked down at his sleeping son and I could almost hear his thoughts for I had seen two of his sons when they were that age and Abe could have passed for either Samuel or James.

After a few moments he turned away and I could see tears in his eyes. Meaning only to comfort him, I laid my hand on his arm. He encased my body in his long arms and I did not resist when he drew me down on my bed. There was a freedom to our lovemaking that had never been there before, perhaps because we were far away from limitations set by people or place.

Later I held little Abe while Mr. Enloe returned to the subject of marriage. He wanted to know if Thomas Lincoln or Floyd Draper had proposed marriage. When I said no, not specifically, he told me what he would offer one of them as my 'dowry.'

"Well," I said, my voice tinged with cynicism, "my choices are rather limited. Not many men would fancy marrying an ex-bondservant with a baseborn child."

Then I apologized and told him that I was sure he would do what was best for little Abe and me.

I saw Mr. Enloe only once more at a gathering in the village. When he told me that he had settled on Thomas Lincoln as the person I should marry, I must confess that I was surprised. Given Mr. Enloe's sense of respectability, I thought he would surely have preferred Floyd Draper. He proceeded to recount all the reasons that Floyd would not make a suitable husband for me. Mr. Enloe's judgment had been my serenity and it appalled me to realize that I questioned it but I was not in a position to turn down his offer of help. I had thought lately that if possible, I would like to raise my son in a place where he could be educated. That would not be possible unless I was married for I knew the mind-set of people in eastern towns, especially if they were very religious. In such places education for my fatherless son would be at best, learning to dig ditches and at worst, forced servitude until he was a grown man.

So, if Mr. Enloe thought Thomas Lincoln was the proper man and was willing to provide my 'dowry' then I would say yes. At least my son would have a legal father.

Abraham Enloe and I said goodbye with a simple nod. I remember thinking three things as he walked away. My estimation of men will always be measured against him, in my heart he will always be my true husband, and I wonder if I will ever see him again.

Thomas Lincoln

 Thomas Lincoln liked to boast that he had been educated in the school of hard knocks. And in the same way he had been taught, so would he teach others, although others usually included women and those unfortunate enough to be smaller than he in physical stature. Lincoln saw nothing wrong with his teaching skills for they had stood him in good stead in the twenty years since his fifteenth birthday when he had soundly whipped his first opponent. He could truthfully boast that neither man nor beast had ever bested him, and it helped that he had his own definition of each.

 Lincoln's physical stature was deceptive for his stocky frame and a tendency to slouch made him appear shorter than his five foot ten. His square face seemed out of kilter, as if it were misshapen somehow, but there wasn't any one thing about it that could be said to be abnormal. His mouth turned down at the corners and thick brows lay so close to his eyes that he appeared to be permanently scowling. He moved with a lumbering walk and kept his short thick hands deep in his pockets when he was not using them. As he walked the lapels of an unbuttoned coat nearly always flapped on each side of his barrel chest.

Thomas Lincoln had left North Carolina because the atmosphere had become a bit too hot. He had created a façade of a simple, honest laborer, uneducated but humble, gruff but kind, with which he moved freely among 'refined' folk, as he sarcastically referred to them. Then the façade had begun to crumble.

He owed money, was wanted for making and selling whiskey without paying federal taxes that had been enacted by Alexander Hamilton in 1791, and was suspected of having helped to break a convicted felon out of jail.

Kentucky seemed the right sort of place for there was no established law as yet and no close acquaintances to lay his history open to the public. He had no trouble finding employment for he had worked at many jobs over the years, drover, teamster, ditch digger, and logger being only a few.

Thomas Lincoln was working with Richard Berry when he first saw Nancy Hanks. She was spreading wet bed sheets over some bushes in the Berry's back yard. He came upon her just as her brat began bawling because of a bee sting. She was a real looker and obviously wise to the ways of the world for she had no husband and, according to talk Lincoln had heard at the tavern, had never had one. He sought a job with Richard Berry so he could get close enough to speak with her for she was seldom in the village. She agreed to walk out with him sometimes but always carried the brat. He knew she had also been friendly with a sickly blond fellow who intended to open a school in the neighborhood, but he did not believe that she could possibly prefer the schoolmaster to him.

Then one day as he sat in the village tavern Abraham Enloe approached him with an interesting proposition. Lincoln could see right away that Enloe was trying to cover his own mistake by making sure the girl was married and out of his way. He agreed to ask Nancy Hanks to marry him because the offer was too good to turn down. He didn't anticipate any problems for she was a sturdy wench and the brat appeared to be healthy. Five hundred dollars would be enough to buy a piece of land he had heard of about ten miles north on Skaggs Trace toward Louisville. A wagon and team were worth almost that much more. As to his promise to provide a good home and look after her and the brat, Enloe would be back in North Carolina and how would he know?

Thomas Lincoln went to see Nancy Hanks immediately and asked her to marry him. She seemed reluctant to say yes right away but promised she would give him an answer soon.

Lincoln looked at her sharply, his dull eyes under sagging brows taking a swift inventory. His eyelids drooped but not enough to hide the cold glint that grew brighter at the thought of the payment Enloe had promised. Could it be that she was thinking of the weakling schoolmaster? Well, he could take care of that.

Lincoln did not have to lay a finger on Floyd Draper. He met him in front of the tavern one day and spoke a few low words in his ear. Draper turned red, then white and the next morning he was on a freight wagon with his few possessions, heading back to a safer climate in Virginia.

Finally Nancy Hanks agreed she would marry Thomas Lincoln but she set the date for March. Then in December she suddenly changed her mind and they were married at the Berry's house in the early morning of January sixth. He had already made the arrangements to take possession of Enloe's payment so the day they were married he walked through Harrodsburg to the Thompson's and demanded his cash, wagon and horses. Enloe's daughter and her husband were some of those Lincoln thought of as "refined" folk. He could read her face and see that she was wondering what her friend was getting into. Well, her opinion didn't matter. In fact, she was welcome to it so long as he got his property.

Lincoln drove back to the Berry's and loaded his wife's possessions on the wagon. The Berrys entreated him to spend the night and leave the next morning so Nancy and the child would not be out in the coldest part of the day. He would not hear of it. Although he was not quite bold enough to voice it aloud to the Berrys, he thought, "I own the both of them and they'll bend to my will now."

They left Harrodsburg and headed northwest on Skaggs Trace. Nancy Lincoln held a quilt around her son and tried to convince herself that she had done the right thing. Thomas Lincoln, hunched beneath a heavy coat, thought of the things he could do with five hundred dollars. One thing he was sure of. It would not be spent pampering his wife and Abraham Enloe's bastard.

Harrodsburg, Kentucky
January 1806

Dear Father,
*   I have not till now had time to answer your letter that arrived in November.*
*   Yes, Arthur continues work on the mill and forge even now for our winter thus far has been very mild. Millstones arrived in early December and Arthur is convinced they are of superior quality. There is much interest in his forge for until it is completed; folks must travel as far as Frankfort for any work other than replacing a horseshoe.*
*   Our life here is much the same day by day. Not dull, but a comfortable sameness with a few welcome distractions now and then. In October our community was favored with a visit by a Methodist minister whose coming had been eagerly anticipated by a few residents who found some tenets of the Presbyterian faith not to their liking. They were mortified to hear Mr. Eustace, a protégé of the esteemed George Whitehead, condemn*

in his sermon what they had mistakenly believed to be Methodist doctrine!

Another event that may interest you is the marriage of Nancy Hanks to Thomas Lincoln on January sixth. The Reverend Jesse Head, a local minister, performed the ceremony. I pray God that Nancy did right in marrying him and that she will not live to rue their union.

Mother, when you or father see fit to answer this letter, please copy and send to me the receipt for the Christmas cake that you had from your mother and your directions for making lye soap. I remember yours as being of a better quality than what is made here.

I send love to my brothers and sisters.

Your affectionate daughter,

Nancy Enloe Thompson

Chapter Eight

<u>Abram Enloe</u>

Upon my return from Kentucky I was determined to conquer my ardor for Nancy Hanks. I returned to a regular schedule in my children's schoolroom, having sadly neglected it in the midst of nearly two years of turmoil.

Felix was occupied in laying the foundation for a political career so my hunting trips were seldom and lonely. William Gwynn was trustworthy enough to make market trips on his own so I spent far less time traveling to Augusta, Charleston, or the settlements and more time making plans for many needed changes and additions to the farm.

Summer and fall swept by and before cold weather set in, Sarah's father and mother braved the elements to make the trip from Puzzle Creek, their one and only time. The New Year began with a fierce snowstorm and then the weather became almost spring like by mid-January. William Gwynn went to Asheville and returned with a letter from our Nancy.

Sarah opened the letter, read it silently, and then handed it to me. Along with information about Arthur's progress on the mill and forge, she informed us of Nancy Hanks' marriage to Thomas Lincoln on January 6, 1806.

I could not speak. I sat for a while in total confusion, then took my musket, saddled a horse, and began riding. Sarah did not try to stop me. I suppose when she read the letter she sensed what to expect.

I felt numb, emotionally and physically, as I rode without any destination in mind. Sometime late in the day, I reached an area of my property that I had never seen. A small meadow, thick with last summer's grass and bisected by a small stream, lay at the foot of a steep hillside that led high up to a cluster of enormous rock cliffs. I unsaddled my horse, turned him loose, and then began to climb. Scattered rocks and dirt beneath my feet almost threw me down several times but I was impervious to any peril. Somewhere near the top I came upon a dark opening that turned out to be a small cave. I entered the darkness and sat down with my face to the back wall. All my heart could project were scenes of Nancy Hanks in Thomas Lincoln's cabin, in his arms, in his bed.

Silent disputation raged in my head.

"I should not have done it. I should have left her alone."

"Yes, but, what could she do on her own?"

"Well, she might have married Floyd Draper if you hadn't interfered."

"But, maybe Lincoln will treat her well."

"You don't know and you don't believe that!"

This internal discourse went on and on and I had no concept of time passing.

Finally, I moved from my cramped position and saw that night had come and gone and the stars were beginning to fade. Mentally and physically exhausted, I stretched out on the dirt floor and went to sleep.

Suddenly I was on the ground in a green meadow wrestling with someone of great strength. His arms were like iron, his hands like animal traps. No matter how hard I tried, he would not allow me to see his face. We fought and fought, rolling in and out of water and over rocks and briars and logs, and finally I was able to turn him on his back. I pinned his shoulders to the ground and when he stopped struggling, I gasped in horror, for I was looking into my own face.

I came awake suddenly to find my entire body drenched in a cold sweat. When I had recovered sufficiently, I descended the rocky slope to the meadow and lay down and drank deeply from the cold stream. I walked back to where I had left my saddle and sat against a tree in the warm midday sun. I had just closed my eyes when a stick broke behind me. I froze, anticipating a bear or mountain lion. My gun was out of reach so I turned very slowly and there was my horse! He seemed none the worse for his night of freedom so I saddled and mounted him, although I knew I could not yet go home. I wandered for two more days and nights, sleeping in rhododendron hells or under rock cliffs, killing and roasting rabbits and pheasants on a stick over a fire when I became weak from hunger. I did not try to think or not to think but let my mind roam where it willed.

The morning I rode into the yard, Sarah came running out of the house in a fury.

"How could you worry us like this? If you hadn't come home today I was going to send William looking for you!"

If she were hoping for a heated dispute she would be disappointed.

"I'm sorry, Sarah. I should not have left the way I did, nor stayed away so long."

After the battle with myself, I came to accept the incontestable fact of Nancy Hanks' marriage, and although I never forgot, I could finally put it behind me, sometimes for weeks at a time.

In the years that followed, Sarah was more than fair to me, perhaps because she finally realized that my attachment to Nancy Hanks would never displace her in my affections and that I would never abandon her and our children. In 1807, our fourteenth child was born, a daughter whom we named Rebecca.

<u>Nancy Hanks</u>

When I agreed to marry Thomas Lincoln I knew my life would change but I could never have foreseen how drastically. I had gotten a glimpse of his true nature when I set the date of our marriage in March. I could sense a fury just beneath the surface, which he managed to keep under control.

"Why wait," he wanted to know. "Let's just get it over with!"

Shortly thereafter, I suspected that I might be with child again from my encounter with Mr. Enloe. A cold fear began to grow in me and I could see only one way out. Thomas Lincoln seemed pleased when I told him in late December that I would agree to bring the wedding forward to the first week in January. He never expressed it but I could see a trace of suspicion in his leaden eyes.

We were married early in the morning and left for the farm on Skaggs Trace before midday. We arrived just as the sun was setting. The cabin, or what remained of it, sat in a field of scrub bushes and last summer's thistles. Several stones had fallen from the chimney and lay forlornly on the ground, the remains of daubing mud frozen to their flat sides. The door hung askance on leather hinges that had dried and cracked almost to breaking. Some sort of bird flapped in our faces as we opened the door.

I lit a candle and was greeted by a hovel not fit for human habitation. The floor was dirt and a stagnant puddle lay beneath a large crack in the roof. The fireplace was filled with half-burnt logs. All manner of old birds nests and other rubbish littered the floor. In despair, I turned to my husband.

"So?" he said. "Clean it up!"

At that moment my future flashed before me and I was to admit many times over the years that my vision had been only too accurate.

While Thomas brought in some of our things, I was able to start a fire among the damp half-burned logs. I found a worn broom made from hemlock branches and cleared enough of the litter to make a space for sleeping. Thomas refused to bring in little Abe's bed so I piled our covers together on the floor and lay down, holding my child close. A sour smell that I recognized as whiskey filled the room and while the fire still burned enough to cast a light, I turned over and saw my husband fast asleep beneath his blankets. I silently thanked God and the whiskey that I was spared, for one night at least, the attentions of Thomas Lincoln.

The second night I was not so fortunate and he took me with a deliberate savagery that left me feeling violated, body and soul. I was to remain grateful in the coming years that Thomas Lincoln was not a man who demanded frequent marital union, for the act never ceased to leave me cold and degraded.

What he did demand was constant control, and to him, violence was the progenitor of total domination. More than once in that first year of marriage I thanked God that I had been mistaken in thinking myself with child. I prayed daily that I would never bring another child into the world.

As months and then years passed, I learned many ways to evade his savage rampages. Mostly they came when he had been thwarted in some way, their importance being of no consequence whatever. A stubborn wagon wheel or a great loss at cards spawned the same kind of fierce outburst that knew no bounds. Were little Abe nearby, Thomas would as leave throw him into the fireplace, as he frequently did our few books if they were in sight.

Abe instinctively managed to stay out of Thomas' way as much as possible. If Lincoln ever showed any consideration for the child, he always followed it by a tirade of curses against Abraham Enloe.

However, our lives, Abe's and mine, were not totally empty of pleasure. Sometimes Lincoln would be gone for days and we would spend our time reading and talking about what little I knew of the world outside our barren circle. We took long walks in the fields and woods and gloried in the harmony of nature, whose only violence came for a purpose. Hard winds stripped trees of rotting limbs and pouring rains cleansed and healed the earth's dry crumbling surface.

During these interludes, I lived. The remainder of the time I only existed and my life was made up of whatever pleased and appeased Thomas Lincoln. Any appeal on my part to patch up the cabin was always met with indifference and at times with unrestrained violence. So, what I could do myself, I did, and the rest remained as it was when we moved in.

Thomas was not a resourceful man but I managed our food supply so there was nearly always something on the table. Our clothes became worn and shabby but I kept hidden the money from my father and Abraham Enloe against a time when we might be truly destitute. It did not stay hidden.

While searching for rags with which to clean his gun, Thomas Lincoln found my little hoard of coins. That was the first time I was truly convinced that he would not hesitate to strike me dead, and indeed, the first time I realized that, had I not my son, I would have wished it so. But I recovered, as I was to do time after time.

By the time Abe was five years old, he was tall for his age. He was already helpful to me in carrying firewood and sometimes half-buckets of water from the spring. He had entered the house with just such a bucket one day and in his haste to set it on the table, tipped it over and splashed cold water on Thomas. He rose with a fury, grabbed Abe by the arm and began slapping him in the face. I jumped between them and tried to loosen his grip, which served only to reinforce his anger. He began to strike at the terrified child with his fists. Finally I was able to break his hold and run with Abe out of the house and into the woods. I held the sobbing child and listened to myself lie, assuring him that everything was going to be all right. The next morning, Thomas acted as if nothing had happened and he left the house without a word.

Abe's arm was grotesquely bruised and swollen and his face and shoulders bore ugly hand and fist marks. By some strange coincidence, that was the day that Nancy Enloe Thompson decided to come for a visit. We had seen each other only in Harrodsburg, mostly at the trading post, since my marriage to Thomas Lincoln.

My old friend had little to say but I could see her eyes taking in the dilapidated cabin and crude furnishings. Then, when she saw the bruises on Abe, her face set in an expression that I remembered well from our childhood. When she hugged us both and left, she still had not uttered more than a dozen words. Intuition told me that she would not visit again.

"Well," I thought. "Alone I have made this hard and cruel bed and alone I shall have to lie in it."

Were it not for my son, I could have freely walked away into the wilderness and died on some barren mountainside. But there was an indomitable quality in him that seemed to offer hope. Of what, I could not envision, but indisputably hope.

Harrodsburg, Kentucky
3 May 1809

Dear Father,

First I will give you our happy tidings. I am again with child and, as ever, I am in good health. The same mid-wife who attended me with Charles will assist me in this confinement that will likely occur sometime in October.

Now, father, I will be as succinct as possible in relaying this appalling message. I have only seen Nancy Hanks in Harrodsburg since her marriage, so two weeks ago I visited her home for the first time.

Nancy and her child are living in the most squalid of conditions. Their one-room cabin has only a dirt floor, there are cracks in the walls and roof, and the chimney is unstable and appears to be in danger of collapsing. Their furnishings, what few exist, are even worse. They sleep on corn shuck mattresses on the floor. Their seating consists of cut logs turned on end. Nancy's threadbare dress was one she wore when we brought her to Kentucky five years ago.

And, Father, that is not even the worst of it. The child had severe bruises that of a certainty did not result from normal boy's play. Nancy had marks on her arm and neck that she attempted unsuccessfully to hide from me.

I report this to you, Father, only because some action must be taken. I know that Thomas Lincoln promised he would care for Nancy and her son and I also know that you compensated him generously. I do not know by what means he can be compelled to abide by that promise but there must be some method.

Mother, I am sorry for the necessity of raising a subject that I know is painful to you but even if Nancy Hanks were a complete stranger I would feel an obligation to help relieve her miserable circumstances in some way.

I send love to my brothers and sisters.

Your loving daughter,
Nancy Enloe Thompson

Chapter Nine

Abram Enloe

Almost four years had passed since Nancy Hanks' marriage and during that time Sarah had almost become her old self again. Our youngest child, Rebecca, was only a year old when Joseph and William came for a short visit in the summer of 1808. They had completed their education, served apprenticeships, and were now about to embark on their professions, Joseph in banking and William in shipping. We had some awkward moments when Nancy Hanks' name arose but we managed to get by without dwelling on the whole story, which was not too difficult. Both Joseph and William were caught up in their own plans and we were caught up in listening to them.

Mary married Felix Walker's nephew in the spring of 1808 and the boys were just in time to see her before she moved to Jonathon Creek. They brought her beautifully designed pewter candlesticks with which she was immensely pleased. After Mary left, Lizzie, now seventeen, became convinced that there would never be a young man for her in Ocona Lufta. And she complained, as much as she dared, about how hard she had to work now that Mary was gone.

Our son David, just a year younger than Lizzie, was very unlike his older brothers. He did well on his schoolwork but what he reveled in was anything out of doors. He loved the farm as I did and nothing pleasured him like a leisurely hunting trip. We were only one day back from just such a trip in spring of 1809 when a letter arrived from our Nancy.

I read it first, and then gave it to Sarah. She read it slowly and handed it back to me. We sat in silence, not knowing what to say to each other. I put the letter in my pocket and went outside. When I came back in, Sarah was still sitting at the table.

"I won't go if you say not, Sarah. I've put you through enough. Just say one way or the other."

She sighed and shook her head.

"Go, for you won't be able to live with yourself if you don't. I can almost feel sorry for her myself."

Lizzie and Samuel, who knew nothing of the reason for the trip, begged to accompany me but I intended to go on horseback to make better time going and returning.

Our Nancy had not expected me so soon and seemed pleasantly surprised. She was plump with child and with a great deal of energy showed me the improvements they had made on their cabin since my last visit. Three-year-old Charles took to me as though we saw each other every day.

The next morning, Arthur took me through the gristmill and the forge, both of which he said were very busy six days a week. He was well aware of the main reason for my visit and before we returned to the house, he cautioned me that Thomas Lincoln had earned quite a reputation in the village for drinking and fighting. I attempted to make light of the warning.

"Well, I won't drink with him and I won't fight with him, so we'll just have to talk."

The next day I left at mid-morning with directions from our Nancy and her unsolicited assurance that she had not exaggerated in her letter.

When I thought I might be getting near, I stopped to ask farmer directions to the Lincoln farm. He looked at me strangely.

"Farm? Humph!"

If I had not been told differently, I would have thought the cabin abandoned. It was set back on the edge of a wood. The field in front had not been plowed in years and had grown up in all manner of thistles, milkweed, and briars.

The cabin itself was sagging on one side and the chimney was dotted with places where the stones had fallen. I dismounted, tied my horse to a post by the only outbuilding in sight, and went up to the door and knocked.

There was no answer but the door swung open of its own volition. The inside was as our Nancy had described it, crude furnishings, bedding on a dirt floor, but painfully clean. With no one about, I resolved to leave but as I started toward my horse, Nancy Hanks appeared carrying a bucket of water. It took a few seconds for her to recognize me and she almost dropped the pail.

Except for a thin streak of gray above each temple and a permanent expression of sadness, she had changed but little. Her piercing gray eyes were the same and my heart surged when I saw them sparkle in recognition. She put down the bucket and approached me with hands outstretched.

"Are you alone," I asked. "I've come to talk with Lincoln."

"Yes," she said. "He won't return until late today and Abe has gone berry picking with one of our neighbors."

As if driven by some unknown force, suddenly we were in each other's arms and nothing else existed. Holding her by the hand, I started toward the cabin.

"No," she said. "Not where we…where he…no, come."

She led me into the wood to a small clearing near a spring. Moss carpeted the ground and rhododendron grew together overhead creating a ceiling of green interspersed with streaks of light.

Later we sat on the edge of the wood on a stone and I begged her forgiveness, as I had done many times before, but this time it was not for my passion but for my part in placing her in such a horrible situation.

"Hush," she said quietly. "Don't be sorry. It never changes anything to be sorry."

She began to tell me her conclusions about her life and I listened in awe and realized more than ever that she had been born for a better life than her present one.

"I've thought a lot lately," she said, "and have come to believe that each of us have three lives. Our first, our birth, when, where, and to whom we are born, is not within our control. Others mostly govern our second life, our forming years. That my mother somehow chose your family was auspicious for me and what I learned in that life prepared me to withstand the life I must live today."

I could but listen to her for I was astonished and could not add to or deny the validity her concept. She continued, her voice growing a little rigid.

"Our third life, the one I am living now, was determined by the choices I made. You never forced me, never unduly pressed me. Our unity was a choice I freely made and I believe it was for a purpose other than our physical enjoyment of each other. I could not go on living if I did not believe that purpose existed. I believe I was put on this earth to bear my son and watch over him until he is beyond my guidance. I still do not regret my mistakes, if they be called so, for I am convinced this fateful tangle of our lives was by design and anything outside that design is pure vanity."

Her face softened as she spoke of her son, our son.

"My life has been determined by my mistakes and any good I ever did is insignificant. My son's life will be defined by his accomplishments. I know not what they will be but I know they will be great. I value more than you can know the years I spent with your family, especially the education that I will work to pass on to my son."

She looked up at me with a slight smile.

"The pain I suffer in this life, and it is not all physical, is God's punishment because I have provoked him by never repenting of my adulterous affection for you."

I was searching my heart for a response when Nancy shaded her eyes and exclaimed, "Here's Abraham now!"

He came across the field and waved when he saw us. He was tall for a five year old and his coloring, hair and eyes would have marked him to any observer as my child. Nancy introduced me as Mr. Enloe and he offered me his hand in an almost adult manner. His expression was intelligent but somewhat somber like his mother's. He went behind the cabin and returned with a bird's nest that contained three bright blue eggs.

"I found it in a bramble. The mother flew away one day and never came back."

I told Nancy to tell Thomas Lincoln I wanted to see him either at home or in the village. As I left, I felt that a part of my heart had been torn away and remained behind me.

The next morning Arthur took me back to the forge where he had encountered a small problem with the furnace. By the time we had sorted it out, our faces were burning, our bodies drenched with sweat. We rode to the tavern, which served locally made ale that was refreshing though not very potent. After resting for a while, Arthur said he must get back to the forge. I wanted to spend some time with our Nancy and my grandson for I would be leaving as soon as I had confronted Thomas Lincoln.

We stepped out of the village tavern still discussing the forge. At that moment, a speeding wagon pulled by a pair of gaunt, raw-boned horses came in sight and we paused at the road's edge to let it pass. Instead, the driver jerked the horses to a silent halt, set the brake, and jumped down. I recognized him at once as Thomas Lincoln and told Arthur to go on, that I would see him later.

I asked Lincoln to follow me to a small grove of oaks across the road from the tavern. We did not need an audience for our discussion. I tried to keep my voice low and clear.

"Obviously, you're aware that I've already been to see Nancy and the boy. I thought you agreed to take good care of them in return for what I paid you."

He came back at me, his voice dripping with barely controlled rage. The heavy muscles of his jaws tightened and drew into ugly knots. His sagging brows drew together above muddy eyes that grew even duller in his obvious hatred of me.

"They ain't starving," he said. "And they got a roof over their heads. And besides, your 'refined' whore and her whelp are mine by law and I'll treat them as I see fit, just like I do them horses over there."

I stepped toward him as he spouted a string of obscenities. Pure rage distorted his features to a mask of fury.

I had not been in a physical confrontation since I was sixteen in Charleston and came upon a man beating a tethered dog with a heavy stick. Even then my success was due more to the energy produced by my anger than by any fighting skills.

Lincoln came at me with his head lowered like a bull, but instead of swinging his fists as I anticipated, he butted me squarely in the stomach. I went down hard but scrambled to rise while I struggled to get air back in my lungs. He came at me again, this time with his fists raised, but I managed to pull aside just as he swung. My long arms helped me to land a solid punch just below his ribs and another lower down before he could get himself set up again.

Thomas Lincoln was much heavier than I and had done plenty of fighting. But he was a heavy drinker besides being a bully who seldom tackled anyone he thought had a chance to best him.

I was ten years older and had no fighting experience, but I had decades of hard physical work behind me, work that built muscle and stamina and wind.

He came at me again and landed a glancing blow to the side of my head. When he backed up, instead of swinging a punch, I rushed at him, caught my arms around his legs and slammed him head first against the trunk of one of the oak trees.

Lincoln's strength seemed to be failing and I tried to hold him down, hoping he would give up. Instead, he put his whole weight against me and twisted his head until we were face to face. He could not free his arms or legs to strike at me but what he did took me by total surprise. His loathsome face came toward mine and I felt his foul breath while his teeth sank deep into the side of my nose.

His action so shocked me that I threw him off violently and he landed hard on his back a few feet away. I scrambled up and took out my handkerchief to catch the blood that was pouring from my nose. Lincoln's clothes were torn and the side of his face was raw and bloody where I had slammed him against the tree but he was motionless. The fight was over.

Suddenly people from the tavern surrounded us. Arthur had not gotten far when he heard the commotion and he returned, leading my horse across the road. I mounted, still holding the handkerchief to my nose. The crowd parted and I had the great pleasure of seeing Thomas Lincoln still lying flat on his back in the dirt.

Not until the next morning did I realize that all I had accomplished was to make life even more miserable for Nancy Hanks and her son. At that moment, I vowed that I would never try to see her again for I could not endure the prospect that I was the cause of ever-increasing pain for her.

Before leaving Harrodsburg, I asked our Nancy to keep back a small sum each month from my share of the profits from the mill and forge. She was to try to get it to Nancy Hanks without Thomas Lincoln's knowledge. Then I implored my daughter, as gently as I could, never to write to me again about Nancy Hanks for there was nothing else I could do. I believe she understood.

I arrived home to find Sarah with child. She hadn't told me before I left because she didn't want me to worry. I appreciated her concern but pondered on the irony that my greatest success seemed to lie in the creation of children.

<u>Nancy Hanks</u>

    I did not expect to ever see Mr. Enloe again but I looked up one day and there he was. Thomas was somewhere helping to build a barn and Abe had gone with our only neighbors to pick berries. I had been walking in the woods, a favorite activity when time allowed, and decided to take a bucket of water on my way back to the cabin.

    Abraham Enloe had started to mount his horse when he saw me. He looked almost the same at forty-nine as when I first saw him. He did not slump like many tall men tend to do as they grow older and his hair still had only scattered streaks of white. Laugh lines at the corners of his eyes gave him a less serious expression than I remembered.

    I held out my hands. After only a few moments of conversation, we were in each other's arms. He sought to go indoors but I led him instead to what I called my magic place in the woods.

After we had exhausted our desires, we sat on a stone at the edge of the woods and talked, at least, I did. I told him that I did not, nor would I ever, regret our union. I told him my belief that our son was destined for greatness, of what manner I was not certain, but greatness, nonetheless.

I was happy that Abe came home before Mr. Enloe left. The look of recognition in his eyes was obvious and he seemed impressed by Abe's intelligence and manners.

Although I was sorry to see him leave, I was glad that Mr. Enloe had come this last time for I knew in my heart that I would never see him again.

Thomas Lincoln

Thomas Lincoln considered himself a 'free' man in the fullest sense of the word. He worked, drank, ate, slept, and fought at his own behest. He worked long enough to have plenty to drink with some left over for food. He slept when and as long as he wanted and demanded that his wife and her child afford him the quiet to do so. He fought only when the advantage was on his side.

Lincoln returned from helping an acquaintance build a barn and found his wife with an almost happy look on her face. The boy also looked cheerful, which belied his usual grave expression.

Nancy gave him Enloe's message. He was silent for a moment and then glared at her through savage eyes.

"I'll see to you when I get back and you can bet on that!"

He had not unhitched the horses and so was able to make his way before long into the village of

Harrodsburg. He pulled into the Thompson's yard just long enough to ask Enloe's daughter where to find her father. Another dash with the already exhausted horses got him to the tavern. Enloe and his son-in-law were just coming out the door.

When Enloe asked him to step across the road, Lincoln smiled to himself.

"Step across the road?" he said to himself. "That's right, and it'll be the last step you take for a long time.

"It was a stunned Thomas Lincoln that only a few minutes later lay in the dirt watching Abraham Enloe's back as he rode away on a fine horse. Lincoln finally got to his feet, shrugged off the few offers of help, and made his way home stunned by his trouncing.

As soon as he had unhitched the horses, he began to berate his wife about Enloe's visit.

"Here today behind my back, and no telling how many other times. Well, it'll all tell in the end. I never told you this before but didn't you never wondered why you ain't come breedin' since we been married? It's because I can't! That's right! I had mumps, a terrible case when I was seventeen and though I've had my measure of wenches over the years, never a one has caught. So, if you do, I'll know where the seed come from and when it was planted, and I'll never let you forget it!"

Harrodsburg, Kentucky
8 November 1816

Dear Father,

At your petition I have not spoken of or reported any information concerning Nancy Hanks for these many years.

I hope you will forgive me now for going against your request. A week ago I received the one and only letter Nancy Hanks has written to me since she came to Kentucky. It was scribbled on a piece of paper that I am sure was torn from the back of a book.

She entreated me to tell you and Mother that she will always be grateful for the years she spent in your home, that she trusts she is no longer a source of disunion between you, and hopes that my brothers and sisters will remember her as kindly as they are able.

She thanked me for the books I sent to her over the years and assured me that they had been put to good use, that her son is a proficient and eager scholar and that her daughter, whom she has inexplicably named Sarah, is also learning to read and cipher.

The cause for the letter became clear when she told me that Thomas Lincoln is moving his family to Indiana in less than a week. She does not know to what part of the state, and will not know until they arrive.

I do not believe Nancy Hanks desired an answer from me and I will respect her wishes for she was once my truest friend and I will remember her as such for the remainder of my life.

Your loving daughter,
Nancy Enloe Thompson

Chapter Ten

Abram Enloe

Our Nancy's letter left Sarah and me in a silent and solemn mood. It was as if a death had occurred of a person whose life had been terribly intertwined with ours and now was gradually disappearing into the annals of the past.

Sarah and I had grown content with each other again for we had come to agree that our future and the future of our children, especially those remaining at home, the last one now five years old, was more important than dredging up an old memory that faded more with each passing year.

Several weeks had passed since our Nancy's letter and one night just as I was falling asleep, Sarah asked, "Abram, why do you suppose she named her child Sarah?"

I answered what I thought was best for all concerned.

"I have no idea."

Much time would pass and I would not even think of Nancy Hanks. Then I would look up and see her face in a cloud and all the old memories would take me again. But at least I could admit that they were only whispers from the past with no more substance than the ever-changing mist in which I saw her face.

For the remainder of my life I continued to be repentant for the weakness to which my flesh was prone but always prayed that my final punishment might be tempered by the fact that my actions were not the result of a cruel and careless heart but of a long-enduring love that was never intended to be.

Nancy Hanks

When Thomas told me that he could not father a child, I could see the twisted delight in his eyes. I remember thinking that when God put him together something went wrong and he allowed Thomas Lincoln to be born without mercy, without conscience, and without the capacity to love.

Well, I did conceive. My daughter was born in the spring of 1810 and to my extreme dismay, Thomas insisted that she be named Sarah, for his mother, he said. But he had never mentioned his mother and I had no way of knowing whether he was sincere or if he somehow knew that Mrs. Enloe was called Sarah. I expect he thought the name would serve as a constant reminder of my infidelity, and it did, although not in an entirely negative manner.

I agreed to name my child Sarah but it was of little consequence. I had never tried to correspond with Mr. Enloe since our last meeting, although Nancy

Thompson, at his behest, had sent me a small amount of money each month through a person she trusted and who managed to always deliver it when Thomas was not around. Then Thomas came home one day and announced that we would be leaving for Indiana in a week. I tore a blank sheet from the back of one of Abe's books, hurriedly wrote to Nancy Thompson and enlisted my neighbor to deliver it without my husband's knowledge.

We left Kentucky this morning bound for I do not know where in Indiana. I dread the trip for Thomas grows angry easily when he is intent on some endeavor. I wish he would not whip the oxen so, for they are slow by nature and can do no better.

I have resolved to tell my son and daughter of their true parentage so they will grow up knowing that they came from families of high quality that valued education, industry, and morals.

I reflect frequently these days on the dream I had when my son was a mere babe where I laid him on a golden altar.

The part that has become clearer over the years, the part I never spoke of to anyone, and indeed, hardly allowed myself to remember, is the end of the dream where I left my child on the altar and walked away from him into the twilight.

I accept that I will never be able to discover the dream's true meaning but maybe someone in the future may do so.

Afterword

<u>April 16, 1865</u>
        In a small town called Puzzle Creek, in the county of Rutherford, in the state of North Carolina, a group of villagers gathered around as a postal clerk read aloud a telegram.
        "President Abraham Lincoln was shot by an assassin and died at 7:22 a.m. yesterday, April 15, 1865."
        A murmur ran through the crowd. One man yelled that it was high time. A woman started to cry and another began to sing a hymn. A very old woman at the edge of the crowd jostled several people before she found someone to answer her.
        "The president, Aunt Polly! Abraham Lincoln has been killed!"
        "Abraham Lincoln, indeed!" she said. "He was an Enloe, not a Lincoln! Why, Nancy Hanks didn't know Thomas Lincoln from Adam when her boy was born. I was twenty years old and I held him while

Nancy Hanks and me got up to sing in the Old Concord Baptist Church!"

No one seemed to be listening so the old woman raised her ancient voice again and pointed down the street.

"I stood right there where the tavern used to be and waved to her as she left Puzzle Creek for the last time with little Abe in her arms!"

The noise of the crowd became louder and a scuffle broke out. A church bell began to toll and in the distance a train whistled low and sad.

And still no one listened. Polly Price walked away from the crowd, muttering to herself.

"Abraham Lincoln, indeed! Abraham *Enloe*!"

~ ~ ~ ~ ~ ~ ~ ~ ~ ~ ~ ~ ~ ~

Author's Note

A huge body of traditional lore has existed for over two hundred years that places our 16th President, Abraham Lincoln's birth in Rutherford County, North Carolina instead of Elizabethtown, Kentucky. This traditional knowledge says that Lincoln was the illegitimate son of a wealthy, respected, well-educated farmer who paid Thomas Lincoln to marry Nancy Hanks and give her child a surname.

Over the past one hundred and forty-four years since Lincoln's death, biographers have largely ignored this story, although no factual evidence and very little hearsay exists, or has ever existed, to place Lincoln's birth in Kentucky.

Apparently these biographers attached a great stigma to the state of illegitimacy, making the ridiculous assumption that it might somehow diminish Lincoln's monumental accomplishments. That attitude exists among many Lincoln scholars, even today.

People in late 19th century Rutherford County had little to say about their native son's actual beginnings. After all, Abraham Lincoln was not thought of with great affection in much of the south at that time. For instance, when he ran for president, Lincoln got only 6 votes in the Kentucky County where he was supposed to have been born.

Around 1895, a man named James H. Cathey decided to set the record straight. He began to gather information on the subject and his book *The Genesis of Lincoln* was published in 1899.

Some 41 years later in 1940, James Caswell Coggins, an attorney and PhD who was also a college president, decided to take up the banner and he wrote *The Eugenics of President Abraham Lincoln.*

Both books are filled with sworn statements, affidavits, and depositions from judges, ministers, teachers, government officials, doctors, bankers, merchants and attorneys, along with the descendants of ordinary folk who lived in the Rutherford area at the time of Lincoln's birth.

These two books kept the story alive and many more have been written, mostly in modern times. My historical novel, *Into The Twilight: A Beginning Disavowed,* is one of those.

Nearly all the characters in *Into The Twilight* are real people. I did not create the Enloe family, Lucy and Nancy Hanks, Felix Walker, Thomas Lincoln, Michael Tanner, or obviously, Daniel Boone. Also, most places are real. I did not create Rutherford County, Puzzle Creek, Duncan's Creek, Ocona Lufta, Jonathon Creek or the settlements of Watauga and Yadkin.

All historical events and dates in the book are accurate. I did a great deal of research on the society of that historical period, on how cabins and other structures would have been built, on agriculture, hunting, weaving, soap and bread making, on modes of travel and historical roads and trails that existed at that time between North and South Carolina. All references to the Revolutionary War are accurate, although nothing exists to prove that Abraham Enloe actually fought at the Battle of Kings Mountain.

I studied a lot of diverse material written by people during the period in which *Into The Twilight* takes place. I can't tell you *how* they spoke, but their style of writing was much more formal than today, even when corresponding with close relatives. Obviously I was not privy to the actual conversations of the characters, so I had to create those.

Also, the traditional stories vary to some extent so I chose to write what I thought most likely happened. However, I wholeheartedly believe that the basis of this story, *which I did not create,* is true - that *Abraham Lincoln, our 16th president, was born in North Carolina and that his real father was Abraham Enloe of Rutherford County.*

Biography

Annis Ward Jackson grew up in the Appalachian Mountains of North Carolina where two branches of her family have lived for nine generations and where storytelling has been a pastime for hundreds of years.

Writing in some form for most of her life, her goal has been to entertain her readers with some stories and inform them with others.

Jackson earned an MA at East Carolina University in Greenville, NC and taught English at Barton College in Wilson, NC. Before returning to the mountains in 1993, she was an English as a Second Language Special Project Director for the NC Department of Community Colleges.

Jackson is an intensive gardener and horsewoman. Both subjects appear frequently in her writing. She lives in the North Carolina mountains with her husband, Kramer, their standard poodles, Daisy and Sophie, and quarter horses, Brick and Sunny.